Books by Elisa Braden

MIDNIGHT IN SCOTLAND SERIES

The Making of a Highlander (Book One)
The Taming of a Highlander (Book Two)
The Temptation of a Highlander (Book Three)—Coming soon!

RESCUED FROM RUIN SERIES

Ever Yours, Annabelle (Prequel)
The Madness of Viscount Atherbourne (Book One)
The Truth About Cads and Dukes (Book Two)
Desperately Seeking a Scoundrel (Book Three)
The Devil Is a Marquess (Book Four)
When a Girl Loves an Earl (Book Five)
Twelve Nights as His Mistress (Novella – Book Six)
Confessions of a Dangerous Lord (Book Seven)
Anything but a Gentleman (Book Eight)
A Marriage Made in Scandal (Book Nine)
A Kiss from a Rogue (Book Ten)

Want to know what's next? Connect with Elisa through Facebook and Twitter, and sign up for her free email newsletter at www.elisabraden.com, so you don't miss a single new release!

Twelve Nights as His Mistress

Elisa Braden

This is a work of fiction. Names, characters, places, and incidents are products of the author's imagination or are used fictitiously and are not to be construed as real. Any resemblance to actual events, locales, organizations, or persons, living or dead, is entirely coincidental.

Copyright © 2016 Elisa Braden

Cover design by Dar Albert at Wicked Smart Designs

Excerpt from *Confessions of a Dangerous Lord* copyright © 2017 Elisa Braden

All rights reserved. No part of this book may be used or reproduced in any form by any means—except in the case of brief quotations embodied in critical articles or reviews—without express written permission of the author.

For more information about the author, visit www.elisabraden.com.

ISBN-13: 978-1-54-812932-3
ISBN-10: 1-5481-2932-1

Dedication

For the Bluestockings.
Because somehow, all along, you knew
a dragon's son must be more than he seems.

Chapter One

*"Heaven knows what he finds so blasted alluring.
Perhaps he has a hidden fondness for peculiarity.
And disaster."*

—The Dowager Marchioness of Wallingham to her boon
companion, Humphrey, while contemplating the mysteries of
obstinate sons, peculiar widows, and courtships that have
clearly run on too long.

November 28, 1818
Fairfield Hall, Suffolk

"Have you ever seen a greater muddle?" Julia Willoughby released a breath and clicked her tongue as she climbed down the library ladder and placed another four books upon the ever-growing pile. "A novel—*fiction*, mind you—shelved beside a reference on landscape architecture. Incredible!" She waved a hand blindly toward the maid seated behind her. "Do not laugh, for I do not jest."

A soft snore was her answer. An hour earlier, Peggy had slumped into the only chair in Lord Dunston's library that remained unencumbered by stacks of books. Apparently, the girl desired slumber more than achieving proper order.

Julia shook her head and placed her hands on her hips, glaring up at the woefully disorganized shelves. "How has he managed all these years?" she wondered aloud. Then she sighed and shrugged. "No matter. By morning, every tome will find its home."

Oh, dear. It must be late. She was rhyming—the peculiar and predictable result of fatigue. Perhaps she should find her bed.

Perhaps she should cease taking liberties with the library of a gentleman who had offered her his hospitality. The Earl of Dunston hosted an annual hunt each year at his country estate, Fairfield Park. She was here as his guest, not his housekeeper.

Lord Dunston is not the gentleman you should be concerned about, she reminded herself.

Such a reminder was unnecessary, of course. Her mission to reorganize an acquaintance's library in the middle of the night was, in truth, merely a distraction from another gentleman. Not an earl, but a marquess.

The man she'd resisted for two long years.

He was here. Well, at least, he was near.

Oh, dear. There went the rhyming again.

She blinked as candlelight flickered and flared where it shone on the dark wood shelves and leather bindings and gold lettering. She covered her face and rubbed her burning eyes with her fingertips. Good heavens, she was tired.

Sucking in a deep breath, she dropped her arms and

gathered her resolve, squinting up at the third shelf from the ceiling.

"Biographies," she murmured to herself, sliding the ladder and beginning her climb. "One rarely has need of biographies."

Golden light flickered madly on a gust of air. A low, smooth baritone barked, "What the devil have you done to Dunston's library?"

She spun. Braced her hand on the ladder's edge. Lost her breath and nearly her footing.

He stalked toward her, looking rumpled. For a man who never looked rumpled, even when soaked to the skin beneath a dripping oak, it was rather alarming.

"Are you mad, woman?"

"Charlie." Her heart breathed the word. That it escaped her mouth with such longing was merely a lack of discipline.

"Answer me."

He was tall—six feet, to be precise—and, since she stood on the lowest rung, his eyes were nearly level with hers as he crossed toward the ladder. Toward the flickering light. Toward her.

Fingers squeezing the cool mahogany of the ladder's rail, she stuttered, "I—It needed sorting."

"By you," he snapped. "At this hour."

She swallowed, her eyes devouring him helplessly: Hair the color of molasses, thick and close-cropped, with a striking bit of silver at the temples. Noble features more bold than handsome—a long, high-bridged nose with a subtle hook at the end; sharp, lofty cheekbones; a chin of rare substance. She'd always thought his profile belonged on a coin.

At the moment, however, he appeared curiously disheveled, his brown tailcoat unbuttoned and carelessly shrugged across athletic shoulders, his cravat missing, his hair mussed. Notable only because she'd never seen him this untidy. And she had known him for years. Two-and-a-half, to be precise. Since before her husband's death.

No, Charlie was not given to disorder. Something was amiss.

As he drew near, she pivoted on the ladder's rung to face him more fully. His eyes, though piercing as ever, squinted with weariness.

"Perhaps I should be asking why *you* are here at this hour," she replied, keeping her voice hushed for two reasons—first, she had no wish to wake Peggy, whose snores huffed in the crackling silence. Second, she could not seem to catch her breath while his face hovered inches from her own. "Should you not have returned to Steadwick Park by now?"

His frown deepened, head tilting slightly. "Dunston and I had matters to discuss. I was leaving his billiard room to return home when I spotted you through the doorway. Is he aware of your little project?"

"No."

"Then, I shall ask again. What do you think you are doing?"

"Putting things in proper order."

"Why?"

"It comforts me."

His hands came up to grip the rails on either side of her. "A bit presumptuous to rearrange a man's library without his knowledge, wouldn't you agree?"

She let her gaze slide along his jaw to his strong, lean neck. What would he do if she simply laid her lips there?

Dratted wayward lust.

"Perhaps," she murmured. "But he will thank me when it is finished."

"Julia."

"Hmm?"

"Look at me."

She did. And what she saw made her burn.

"Neither of us need suffer this way," he rasped, those jewel-green eyes flashing like a brushfire across her skin. "If you seek comfort, I shall happily provide."

Inside, every womanly part of her groaned and ached. This was why she was awake. Restless. Anxious. Because of him.

He was not supposed to be here. She'd only attended Dunston's hunting party in a halfhearted effort to secure a husband. She hadn't realized Charlie's preferred country estate neighbored Fairfield Park. Or that he'd appear like a vision from her most scandalous dreams in Lord Dunston's drawing room. Or dine five chairs away from her at Dunston's table. Or discover her here in Dunston's library. Sorting. Struggling to bring order to the chaos inside her.

Mahogany rails squeaked beneath the pressure of his grip as he moved in tighter, warming her front with his heat. "I can feel your need, despite your refusal to acknowledge it." Breath brushed her throat. His scent—soap and water and the faintest hint of cognac—weakened her like fire devouring wood. "What is the point of denying ourselves?"

Her eyes drifted closed. What was the point, indeed? Only that she loved him. Loved him more than she'd ever loved anyone, including her husband. Arthur. Dear, dear Arthur, who had slowly grown sadder and more resigned as the years of their marriage had passed.

Embers cooled enough for sanity to return. "Please," she whispered. "Let us not revisit old ground. Surely you cannot have forgotten the disaster we are together."

"A few mishaps do not make us a disaster." He bit upon the final word with disgust.

Opening her eyes, she saw frustration creasing his dark, beloved brow. She wanted to stroke him there. Ease him. Kiss him.

She could not. For his sake, she could not.

"Charlie." Once again, his name escaped without her permission, breathless and needy. She pressed her lips together and braced herself to refuse the man she loved for what she hoped was the last time. She could not bear to keep doing it. Every time cut her so deeply she was surprised she had any blood remaining. "Mishaps? Our first drive in Hyde Park together ended with both of us drenched to the skin."

"I apologized five separate times on that excursion—"

She sighed. "Six. And it is not about apologies."

"You and your gown dried without incident. The hinge on the barouche's top was repaired the next day."

"Yes, but my bonnet had to be discarded."

"I offered to replace it. Besides, that was two seasons ago."

"Do you mean the same season when you believed those scurrilous rumors about my supposed infidelity with a coachman and two stable hands? That season?"

"Again, I apologized for—"

"And let us not forget the incident with Lady Randall's pug."

"Entirely Lady Randall's fault. Her failure to control that fat little menace—"

"Yet another bonnet I was forced to burn." She sniffed and swallowed her amusement. "Those sorts of stains never come out, you know, and even if they did, the smell would not."

Jaw flexing, he replied, "Accidents happen. It does not mean we are cursed, damn it."

"Last season, we nearly died when you lost control of your phaeton on Rotten Row."

His substantial chin jerked upward as though tugged by one lifted brow. "The reins slipped from my hand after you told me you planned to marry another man." The low, seething words evidenced the strength of his continued fury. Before this evening, it had been the last time she'd seen him, that day in the park when she had done what was necessary—what was best.

Swallowing, she focused on his lips, normally thin and defined, currently tight, flat, and grim. "We do not belong together, Charlie. Nothing about this is right."

"You are wrong."

"I am sensible."

"Bloody hell, Julia. You persist in punishing us both for feelings we did not act upon—"

"It was a betrayal of Arthur. Of my vows to him."

"You poured my tea. We sat in silence together. Nothing

more happened while you were married."

She lifted her eyes to his. "You know better than that."

His gaze was explosive. Lustful. Just as it had been that day in Arthur's rented London house. She remembered every moment—the tremulous yellow light through the drawing room windows. The weight of the quiet, elegant, powerful marquess's green gaze upon her throat. The strange yearning to touch him.

No, they had not acted upon the attraction, merely sitting in thick silence on a white settee while Arthur retrieved some papers.

But the feelings had been real. Palpable.

They had shaken her until everything she knew about herself grew foreign and uncertain. She had pleaded with Arthur to let her leave London early, return to Bedfordshire. Where she was safe. Where she could organize Willoughby Manor to her liking and pretend the world was not filled with volatile longings for a man who was not her husband.

Then, her husband had died. Broken his neck in a carriage accident on his way home for Easter. And she had mourned. Regretted. Stewed inside a broth of grief and shame.

A year later, visiting London with Arthur's young heir and his mother, she'd encountered the object of her forbidden fascination again. He had pursued her. Courted her. Convinced her to entertain the notion of marriage—to him. Until she'd been reminded of the selfishness of her desire for him and all the reasons she must let him go.

"I shall not apologize for wanting you," he said now, his coat brushing her breasts. "I am not sorry."

"Let me down," she whispered, staring at his chin.

"No."

"I have work to do."

"We are not finished with our conversation."

She gritted her teeth, needing an escape. He was too close. Too tempting.

If he will not let me down, then perhaps I should go up.

Desperately, she twisted, grasping the ladder's rail, her slippers spinning on the rung until her back was to him. Her hip bumped him hard, her elbow colliding with his shoulder.

But it was no escape, for he was not deterred. His arm came hard around her waist, forcing her back into his body. That long, lean, athletic body.

"Where do you think you can hide from me, Julia?" The words were more heat than sound against her nape. "Here in Dunston's library? A dower cottage in Bedfordshire? There is nowhere I would not find you."

This was the man only Julia seemed able to see. His mother's son. Fierce and determined. A dragon in his own right. He wanted her. She knew that. Perhaps he even loved her, as she did him. But wanting something—even loving something—did not make possessing it the proper choice.

And yet, her body did not care a whit. It, too, clawed to give him everything he asked.

The battle was killing her.

"Please, Charlie," she panted, rocking her forehead against cool wood. "I need you to let me go."

He did not. Instead, one hand loosened from the ladder to stroke her neck, those long, beautiful fingers curling around her throat and beneath her jaw in a possessive caress. "You cannot hide from me. And you cannot hide from this. Marrying some aged country squire will only worsen the longing."

Her hips now cradled his arousal, the lustful hardness pressing insistently against her backside. While her arousal was less noticeable, it was no less potent. Every breath, every word, every stroke of those masterful fingers upon the soft flesh just beneath her earlobe intensified the ache in her belly, the painful sensitivity of her breasts, the bone-melting heat in her arms and spine and legs.

"He can never quench your appetite, Julia. Do you know why?"

She moaned. It was the only answer she had.

"You hunger for me alone." The hard arm around her waist gripped and tightened. Soft lips nibbled her neck. "You believe you can be content managing his house and pouring his tea and tidying his waistcoats. But all the while, you will be starving."

She gasped and jerked as his hand dropped from her throat to cup her breast, releasing a torrent of fire from its needy center.

"For this." With the gentlest pressure, he squeezed her nipple.

This time, her body fell against him fully, her head lolling back onto his shoulder, her hands reaching up to grip his hair. Her hips writhed against him.

Needing. Needing. Needing to stoke him the way he had done to her.

"For every bloody thing I can give you. All the things he never will."

"Oh, God above," she groaned. "You must stop, my love."

She felt his grin grow against her skin. "A rhyme. It appears I am doing rather well."

"M-my lady?" The rusty inquiry came from behind them, from a shadowed chair where her maid had fallen asleep.

Asleep no longer, it seemed.

"Peggy. His lordship was just helping me—er, assisting me with the ladder."

A sniff. A shuffle of skirts. "If you say so, my lady. May I find my bed now?"

Thankfully, in addition to being obsessively diligent with scrubbing and dusting, the maid was both incurious and discreet, all reasons why Julia had selected her from Willoughby Manor's staff to serve as her maid-of-all-work.

Presently, Julia cleared her throat, clutching the ladder's rails once again while Charlie's hands and arms and heat slowly withdrew. "Yes, of course," she answered the girl. "It's very late."

The sound of the library door closing upon Peggy's hasty exit set Julia in motion. She clambered down from the ladder and spun to face him. He now stood six feet away, his back to her, his hand braced on the dark wood mantel while he stared down into the low flames.

Taking the opportunity to gather her wits and her resolve, she swallowed and smoothed the hair above her ear. It had come loose while she writhed against him.

"I gave you my answer in London, Charlie," she said in the awkward hush. "I have not changed my mind."

His head shook. Without turning around, he answered, "Then why did you come here? You must have known—"

"No. I assumed you would winter at Grimsgate." The sprawling Northumberland castle was his ancestral home, the seat of his marquisate. Steadwick Park was merely a secondary property, albeit home to his renowned stables. Charlie was widely regarded as having the finest collection of horseflesh in England.

Perhaps she should have known he would be there. And, very well, perhaps a part of her had hoped he would be—the rebellious, improper, unruly part. Dash it all, she would quell that part into silence if she had to spend the next fortnight reordering every room in Lord Dunston's house.

Golden firelight played with the silver at Charlie's temple and knife-edged cheekbone as he turned to glare at her. "If you believe I will allow you to marry a daft, disheveled old widower, you are out of your head."

The thread of steel in his voice spoke more clearly than his words. It ran her clean through, turning her skin to gooseflesh. Most people saw this man as quiet, patient, distinguished. Some might even regard him as unassuming. But that was only because his mother was a ferocious, manipulative dragon, and by comparison, he appeared quite tame.

As Julia had learned well, however, appearances were deceiving.

"It is not for you to say whom I shall marry." Even to her own ears, her voice lacked conviction.

"You will marry me."

His low words sank into the heart of her. Made her ignite from the inside out as though his hands and lips had never left.

"Your refusal is nonsense, Julia." Now his eyes were upon her, narrowed and glittering. Tortured. Resentful. "I've given you months to reconcile whatever fears have sent you fleeing from me. No one can deny I have been patient. But the time for patience is over."

The air inside her felt like it was expanding, pressing outward against her ribs and skin. She had expected him to accept her refusal graciously, as any gentleman should. She had not expected this, although perhaps she should have.

"Charlie—"

"Enough." His voice was clipped and harsh. "We have done everything your way for two bloody years. It is well past time for me to take matters in hand."

Her heart throbbed and pounded as she watched him turn on his heel and stalk toward the library door. "What does that mean?" she whispered as shadows at the edge of the room swallowed his tall, lean form. Louder, she insisted on knowing. "Charlie. What do you intend to do?"

She could not see his expression, but after a gust fluttered the firelight, she felt him pause, felt his eyes lay upon her like a flame. "The hunt lasts a fortnight. Ample time to persuade an intelligent woman to see reason, wouldn't you say?"

A protest was still in her throat when she felt him leave. Rather than release it, her eyes drifted shut, squeezing as hard as her fists.

Oh, dear heaven. She could not do it again. Pretend not to love him. Pretend she did not wish to be his wife. She simply could not. It had torn a hole inside her the first time.

Her eyes flew open, searching the room for an answer. She found stacks of books amid the flickering light, organized into categories and arranged by subject, then author, then title. She breathed in the scent of leather, paper, dust, and the faint, acrid odor of the fireplace. Distantly, she felt her hand straying to her belly, forming a claw. With a grunt of frustration, she forced her arms back to her sides.

"Biographies." The word was a feathery rasp uttered through a tight throat. She eyed the double stack on the leather chair, then the third shelf from the ceiling, then the mahogany ladder. And, with a great effort, she willed herself to move. "We shall begin with biographies."

Chapter Two

"Persistence is laudable, Humphrey. If, however, your endeavors are limited to chasing your quarry about the countryside whilst being forever denied your prize, I fear your behavior must be described in a far less flattering fashion."

—THE DOWAGER MARCHIONESS OF WALLINGHAM to her boon companion, Humphrey, upon said companion's vain yet persistent pursuit of a wily and elusive squirrel.

"SHE HAS DISMANTLED MY LIBRARY." HENRY THORPE, THE EARL of Dunston, was an affable fellow—dapper and devil-may-care. A man fond of waistcoat variety and known for droll wit. In other words, one not much given to grumbling. But his tone on their early-morning bout of pheasant hunting rang with annoyance. "I've yet to locate *The Life of Samuel Johnson*. I was only halfway through it. Bloody hell."

Hefting four braces of limp birds and watching his breath plume white to merge with the morning's mist, Charles continued trudging across a field dotted by brown grass and frozen mud without answering. What could he say? The woman was mad. And maddening.

And beautiful.

Intellectually, he knew she was not the *most* beautiful female he'd ever seen. That distinction belonged to the recently wed Lady Tannenbrook. But these were technicalities. To him, Julia was enchantment itself.

Every rhyming, organizing, maddening inch of her.

"Have you nothing to say?" Dunston pressed. "She is here because you demanded I invite her and that whelp, Willoughby." The dapper earl shook his head and huffed a disbelieving chuckle. "A new, obscure baron with appalling Whig sympathies, *and* his mother, *and* his cousin's dowager widow. Ridiculous. Why did I listen to you?"

Their return journey to Fairfield Hall after a successful morning of fowling had begun with this subject, and the man had not yet ceased his nattering complaints.

Dunston's excellent spaniel trotted between them, the brown, silken fur of her ears the same chestnut as her master's hair. Around them, gray mist swarmed dun fields and listless leaves into stillness. Only the crunch of their boots, the huff of their breath, the panting joy of a chestnut spaniel, intruded upon the silence.

Oh, and Dunston's incessant carping. Mustn't forget that.

Patiently, Charles waited for the younger lord's ire to run its course. He had always liked the man, and despite the odd bout of ill humor, Dunston was exceedingly amiable and far cleverer than he appeared—fine qualities to find in a friend and neighbor.

Exasperation was understandable, he supposed. All of society knew Charles Bainbridge, the fourteenth Marquess of Wallingham, had attempted—and failed—to woo the Dowager Baroness Willoughby into marriage. He'd pursued her with patience and persistence, as he did most things. Unfortunately, his efforts had resulted in several disastrous scenarios and more than one ruined bonnet, but not, unfortunately, in marriage. That, too, was well known among the ton, and he could not blame Dunston for his skepticism. What else was he to think when a seemingly sane friend plied him with French cognac before demanding he alter the guest list for his annual hunt?

Charles was not the obsessive sort, nor was he particularly manipulative. He was rational. Calm. A man well past the first flush of youthful indiscretion—although he'd never had a flush of indiscretion, youthful or otherwise—and he took pride in maintaining command of himself.

Except in regards to a certain widow. She had driven him half-mad.

No, Dunston could not be expected to understand. Julia Willoughby, Lady Willoughby, was extraordinary. No one could match her, and he had no intention of letting her baseless doubts keep them apart.

Further, he refused to think of her as a dowager. Dowagers were women like his mother—white-haired and creased with age, a seventy-two-year-old matron who reigned like a dragon queen over her golden parlor on Park Lane.

Not Julia. Her hair shone like a field of wheat. Or his favorite new dun colt, Icarus. Or the cheesecakes his cook made to accompany Friday supper.

Perhaps it was just as well he'd never tried his hand at poetry, but the fact remained, she was not old. Her hair was blonde with no threads of gray, no loss of luster.

Additionally, when she smiled, the corners of her eyes crinkled becomingly. Otherwise, she had not a single unbecoming line that he could discern. She was only thirty, after all.

Strictly speaking, she *was* a dowager, he supposed. Her late husband's cousin, Miles Willoughby, had inherited the title two years earlier, and the boy's recent marriage necessitated a distinction between the current and former Ladies Willoughby. But, to Charles, she was simply Julia. The woman he intended to marry.

If only she would bloody well agree to it.

As they passed through an area of low brush, Dunston transferred his fowling piece from the crook of his elbow to his shoulder with ghostly ease. Though Charles was a fair hand at hunting, himself, he had long marveled at the earl's otherworldly tracking instincts and deft handling of weaponry. In Dunston's hands, everything from long guns and pistols to swords and knives became an extension of his limbs. For a supposed gentleman of leisure—one who had never been a soldier—such expertise was unusual.

Presently, Dunston slanted him a sideways glare and raised a single chestnut brow as they began ascending a shallow rise. "One hopes your plan to woo her away from Sir Mortimer surpasses your previous efforts. I'd hate to think all this inconvenience has been for naught."

Charles frowned at the reminder. He'd harbored no prior enmity for Sir Mortimer Spalding. The doddering, slovenly old baronet could have remained a calcified relic at his home outside Cambridge until the sun winked out of existence, for all his consequence to Charles's life.

Except ... ah, yes. Except, except, except.

Except *she* had decided Sir Mortimer Spalding—inconceivably—would make a superior husband to the fourteenth bloody Marquess of Wallingham.

An outrage. That's what it was. The man was fifteen years her senior with three grown sons and a collection of botanical treatises less dusty and more riveting than he was.

"She will marry me," Charles said, low and grim. "He can scarcely keep from nodding off after supper at his age."

"He is not much older than you, Wallingham."

Annoyance at the reminder pulsed through him. He absently stroked the silvering strands at his temple. He was forty. Hardly in his dotage. And nothing at all like Spalding. For one thing, the man's entire head was gray and perennially unkempt. For another, the baronet could scarcely sit a horse without fumbling for his quizzing glass.

He glared in Dunston's direction, taking care not to reveal too much. "Regardless, they are ill suited. It will not stand."

"How do you propose to prevent the match?" Dunston challenged. "Appears she has made her choice. Best learn to accept it."

Charles halted in place, waiting for Dunston to do likewise, which he did, turning to face him with a frown of consternation and a rhythmic exhalation of steam. His spaniel similarly spun and came back to sit beside his knee, gazing up at her master adoringly.

"The lady is mine," Charles uttered, the words as cold and dark as the ground beneath his soles. "Perhaps not yet in name, but in all ways critical to a man's purpose, she belongs to me." All but one, that was—an oversight he intended to rectify without delay.

Chestnut eyebrows arched above twin sparks of amusement. "I see."

"No, you do not. But one day, you will, and then I shall be the one laughing."

"You might be surprised by what I understand, Wallingham. So, have you considered what you will do if she fails to accede to your greater wisdom? Perhaps she simply doesn't feel the same attachment."

"She does. She is fighting it. God knows why."

"Well, well." Dunston ran a hand over his mouth before shaking his head in obvious mirth. "This is all rather ... unexpected."

Charles sniffed. "How so? It's been two years."

"Oh, not that you want her. That much is dreadfully obvious. No, I was referring to this streak of ruthless certainty you're exhibiting. Puts me in mind of someone. Now, who could that be?"

Dunston was mocking him. He did not appreciate it. "Leave my mother out of this."

The earl laughed as though Charles had made a hilarious jest. "How can I, when she has made such an extraordinary appearance at my hunt, all without leaving Northumberland?"

"I am nothing like her. You are daft."

Peals of laughter broke from the other man's lips in puffs of vapor as his free arm came around his own ribs and six dead pheasants shook next to his thigh.

Disgusted by the display, Charles started past him, swiping at a tall bit of grass as he made his way toward a hedgerow fifty yards ahead.

Behind him, he heard a final crack of laughter, then a brief whistle, then Dunston's sardonic attempt at an apology. "For God's sake, man. Don't act as though I've insulted your manhood," he called. "I happen to admire your mother. She's bloody formidable."

Charles did not slow his stride. Let the cheeky lord sprint to catch him.

Dunston soon did. "Come now, Wallingham. It is only that I misjudged your character. Such errors occur infrequently, of course, but they do occur. I mistakenly thought you rather ..."

This time, Charles did slow. "Rather what?"

A shrug. A twist of amused lips. "Restrained. Sober. Thoughtful."

"Tedious, you mean."

"No. Merely a man who prefers to control himself rather than others. Quite the opposite of your mother, actually."

"Precisely." Charles's frown deepened. "And?"

Again, Dunston shook his head. "I am delighted to find

otherwise, that is all." At Charles's bristling displeasure, Dunston held up a hand. "You disguise it admirably. Not to worry. I am certain no one else suspects. Well, perhaps Lady Willoughby. She has, after all, been the target of your ... determined focus, shall we say?"

"You are talking rubbish."

"No. I am quite good at this."

"At what?"

A harder, more serious glint entered Dunston's eyes. "Unearthing one's essential nature."

"Stuff and nonsense," he retorted. "My assertion that Lady Willoughby should be my wife is a rational conclusion based upon two years' acquaintance and pursuit of said goal. For her to marry anyone other than me is both absurd and grotesque."

Dunston gave a long blink. "Ah, yes. Perfectly logical."

"I shall prevent such an atrocity with my last breath."

"Atrocity?"

"Fortunately, my demise is unnecessary. She will come round. I shall see to it."

"Hmm. Indeed. And if she does not?"

Suddenly, Charles felt the tension in his body keenly. Fists clenched, jaw sore from grinding, abdomen tight over a burning stomach. He knew what this was. And he liked it even less than being compared to the Dowager Marchioness of Wallingham.

But a man must do what a man must do.

"I shall see to it," he repeated, low and resolute.

Dunston's grin split and spread like candlelight through a cracked door. "There it is," he breathed. "The dragon. How could I have missed him all these years?"

Deciding it was best to ignore his demented friend, Charles snorted and stomped forward, ready to be warm again.

Ready to see Julia again.

As he passed, Dunston clapped his shoulder jovially then came into step beside him. Charles expected further daft assertions about his "essential nature," but the earl opted for companionable silence, the spaniel bounding behind them with a yip.

Unfortunately, in the quiet, his thoughts became a fearsome noise.

And if she does not feel the same?

She does, he had answered Dunston. But was it true?

He glanced down at the slavish creature between them. The dog's tongue lolled merrily, her dark eyes repeatedly returning to Dunston to ensure he had not forgotten her over the previous thirty seconds.

Was Charles the spaniel, trailing after Julia with unseemly devotion, eager for any sign that she shared a similar attachment?

Am I a fool? Or worse, am I repeating Mother's mistakes, insisting the rest of the world conform to my liking?

Suddenly, as they passed through the hedgerow gate and Fairfield Hall came into view, he could not stop himself from wondering. Had he miscalculated their connection? He had offered her everything, and she had refused him. He'd been so shocked, he'd lost control of a carriage for the first and only time in his life, his fingers numb and useless.

But before that moment, before that day, she had felt it, too. He knew that. He'd seen it. And he remembered. Oh, yes, he remembered every bloody moment of their time together.

Perhaps all he must do, then, was remind her.

Watching the spaniel bound happily beside Dunston's knee—ears flying, tail wagging—he felt a small smile play about his lips.

Yes. A reminder was long past due.

Chapter Three

*"Pray, recall how this began. With foolishness.
Followed by calamity. One hopes even a mind as feeble
as yours will begin to sense a pattern."*

—The Dowager Marchioness of Wallingham to her nephew
upon receiving notice of his reinstatement to Oxford after lengthy
negotiations and harsh recriminations.

Two years and nine months earlier – February 1816
London

As Charles handed his hat and gloves to Arthur Willoughby's butler, he glanced around the entrance hall. The walls were white-paneled. The floors polished wood. A rented house, obviously. Lord Willoughby did not have the means to purchase a London residence, even one so small as this. But he was surprised by how elegantly appointed the space was—a marble-topped mahogany table against one wall, centered by a blue-and-white vase of white lilies and yellow roses. Above the table, a small painting of a verdant summer valley glowed inside a frame of dark walnut. Like the table and vase and flowers, the painting was exquisitely simple, neither large nor ostentatious, but imbued with quality. Whoever had selected these pieces possessed a talent for making the most of limited resources.

"This way, my lord," the butler's nasal tones intruded on his thoughts.

Charles nodded and followed the dark-clad man down a corridor and up the staircase to the first floor. Along the way, he could not help noting the clean, quiet orderliness of the house. No stray drips of wax upon the gleaming floors. No dust crowding the corners of the stair treads. It was spotless. Well lit. Pleasantly hushed. Even his mother would be impressed.

The butler showed him to the drawing room, standing to one side as he swept the door open. This room, while likely the largest room in the house, would have fit neatly inside his library at Wallingham House, and thrice inside his drawing room. However, like the entrance hall, its restrained elegance was masterful—paneled walls painted a muted blue-green, twin settees upholstered in white-on-white stripes, a low table between them topped by a silver tea tray, a gleaming pot, and three white china cups. It invited a man to rest and sip and breathe freely.

"Wallingham! Dashed good to see you, man." Arthur Willoughby strode toward him from the direction of the gold-draped windows, his spectacles flashing in the early spring light. Although neither tall nor big, Willoughby always gave the impression of leashed energy and restless drive. He was perhaps a year or two younger than Charles, his light hair receding from a high forehead, his small-boned frame trim and clothed predictably in a dark-blue coat, gray waistcoat, buff trousers, and white cravat.

Willoughby offered his hand and Charles shook it without hesitation. The man might be a Whig with overweening political ambitions, but throughout their acquaintance, he'd always been forthright, which was more than could be said for many others who sought Charles's support.

"My thanks for the invitation, Willoughby," Charles replied, nodding toward the tea tray. "Inveigling my cooperation for a bill that opposes our government might require more than a bit of tea and conversation, however."

Willoughby's grin grew, and his eyes wandered past Charles's left shoulder. "Perhaps a dose of charm will do. That is why I asked my wife to join us, is it not, dear?"

Swiveling on his boot heel, Charles saw Lady Willoughby approaching from the direction of a mahogany writing desk in one corner of the room. Having conversed with her on two previous occasions, he found her quite an appealing woman—intelligent, serene, warm. Their last conversation had been at Lady Reedham's supper, where they had been seated together, spending hours discussing everything from his love of riding to her fondness for "proper library organization." A bit bewildered by her passion for the subject—he'd never thought deeply about the importance of categorizing first and alphabetizing second—he'd nonetheless found her explanations both lucid and persuasive.

And, quite unexpectedly, he'd been enchanted.

Perhaps it had happened when she'd stopped, blushed, and laughed at herself for "going on about such a tedious subject, my lord." Yes, perhaps that was the moment.

Additionally, her beauty grew the more one gazed upon it. Upon first viewing, for example, her hair was merely a medium shade of blonde. In the candlelight of Lady Reedham's dining room, however, he'd noted both lighter and richer tones amidst the color, champagne and honey by turns. Now, this morning, he also saw her eyes were more amontillado sherry than amber cognac. And their shape curved along with her lips, forming beguiling crinkles at the corners. Her nose came to refined point. Her smile was wide and bright, her jaw surprisingly strong. She was an attractive woman. No, a *captivating* woman. Willoughby was right to employ her in his campaign to garner Charles's cooperation.

"Lady Willoughby," he murmured, bowing deeply as a sign of his admiration.

She nodded, dimples showing as she grinned her welcome. "I must admit, Lord Wallingham, my husband did not find it an easy task, luring me to London."

He felt an answering smile tugging at his own lips. "No?"

"Mmm. I prefer the country. But I am most pleased I decided to come, if only to have made your acquaintance. It has been ages since I enjoyed a conversation more than the one we shared at the Reedham supper. Even though I know Willoughby intends to monopolize your time today with political matters, I am delighted you are here."

In anyone else, he would have found her flattery false and ingratiating. But Julia Willoughby emitted sincerity the way a rose emitted perfume. Naturally. Effortlessly. Whether it was real, he could not say. It *felt* real. "I can only hope to earn such regard, my lady," he murmured.

"Shall we sit?" she inquired brightly, gesturing toward the settees.

He offered his arm. After the briefest hesitation, she took it, her fine-boned hand settling upon his sleeve.

Somehow, he found himself seated beside her, watching those hands pour his tea with neat precision while Willoughby expounded upon all the reasons to repeal the property tax that had been levied during the war.

Charles nodded his thanks and took a sip before meeting Willoughby's avid gaze. The other man sat forward on the opposite settee, eyes firing behind his spectacles. "The petitions that have been read in the House of Lords are only the beginning, Wallingham. You must realize this. Agriculture has been hard hit of late. Farmers are suffering. Your own estates must feel it. These onerous taxes cannot continue, particularly given that the people were promised they would end upon Bonaparte's defeat. It has been nearly a year since Waterloo."

The tea was good, he noted. Strong and fragrant and perfectly steeped. Superior quality, if he did not miss his guess. "The war was costly," he said. "Our debt is a burden of some enormity. If not income taxes, then what?"

Their discussion continued for another hour. Charles was uncertain why he bothered arguing the Exchequer's case, given he had already decided to lend his support to the tax abolitionists.

He liked sitting in this room. He liked the tea—he was on his third cup. Most of all, he liked the still, quiet presence beside him.

She smelled of roses kissed by lavender, soft and cool and floral like the south garden at Grimsgate.

Long ago, he had decided never again to marry, never again to crave the solace of domestication. But this was lovely. *She* was lovely. Perhaps his mother had not been entirely wrong, galling though it was to admit. Perhaps he should reconsider taking a wife.

Only if she is as splendid as Lady Willoughby. The thought gave him pause. Were an enchanting smile and a perfect cup of tea worth the risk of returning to the hell he'd once inhabited?

"I see you doubt my claims, Wallingham." Willoughby popped up from his settee like a hound gamboling after a fallen quail and paced toward the drawing room doors, holding a finger up behind him. "I have reports from three counties that you must read. I'll be but a moment."

Blinking, Charles swallowed his last sip of tea and leaned forward to place his empty cup on the tray.

Her hands came to the pot automatically.

Without a thought apart from preventing her filling his cup a fourth time, his own fingers brushed her knuckles where she squeezed the pot's silver handle. Oddly enough, the touch of his skin against hers startled him, as though he'd performed some untoward intimacy.

Reaching beneath her skirts to stroke her inner thigh, for example. Or running his thumb across the bead of her nipple.

Holy God, where had these thoughts come from?

He withdrew his hand as though she'd scalded him. Which, in a sense, she had.

His eyes strayed to her bodice. She wore fawn silk, simple and unadorned. Modest, even. But the scooped neckline further filled with a lace fichu could not disguise the fullness of her breasts. Rather shocking fullness, now that he gave them a proper look. Round and full and lush—a rarity on such a slender woman.

Unable to stop himself, he pictured them bare. Her nipples would be the color of peaches, he predicted. Blushing peach like her lips.

"M-my lord, would you ... would you care for anything more? I am happy to pour."

He swallowed, watching those lips form words, watching the gentle morning light color peach to silvery pink, turn milky skin to luminous pearl. She had a mole just beneath her ear, a russet spot on her otherwise perfect neck. But even her imperfection was perfect. He could imagine pressing his lips there as he bent her forward and thrust inside her.

Stop this. She belongs to Willoughby. You do not dally with ladies of quality, much less those married to Whig barons. His eyes would not obey him. The strange fire of the silence and this room and her scent and his lustful imaginings blended into a heady elixir he'd never experienced, even with his more adventurous mistresses.

Could perfectly poured tea be an aphrodisiac? Perhaps it was not the tea, but the pourer, for she had him seized inside the most erotic moment of his life.

He watched as those nipples he'd been imagining thrust outward against silk, protesting their confinement through layers of corset and shift. Blood rushed loudly in his ears, pounding inside his cock.

Something had disturbed her breathing, caused it to quicken. Those lushly rounded breasts rose and fell with erratic bursts. If he could hear anything beyond his own thundering blood, he supposed he might hear her panting. For his own part, he managed to control his breathing.

But not his eyes. They wanted their fill. They wanted her skin and her lips and those sweet peach nipples. Were they peach? He wanted to know.

This was wrong. He should leave. Willoughby would return soon. Surely a man would notice the once-dignified Marquess of Wallingham contemplating the color of his wife's nipples while sporting a fully sprung staff inside his trousers.

Yes. He should leave.

His hand, quite of its own accord, stretched from its position beside his leg, widening across white-striped upholstery until his smallest finger felt the edge of fawn silk. Felt the heat of her thigh warming him just at the tip.

He should leave. Now. And he would. He would.

I will, damn it.

He watched her eyes close. Watched her tongue dart out to wet her lips. Watched that long, pearlescent throat ripple on a swallow.

Distantly, he heard boots striking polished wood planks, the sounds growing louder as they approached the doors.

Charles had lived a long life of outward restraint. His mother sought to control him. Men like Willoughby sought to influence him. Ladies sought to marry him, though that had waned over time. All of it, he had borne with patient endurance and ruthlessly directed will. But right now, in the elegant confines of a hushed drawing room, inside a rented town house on the outskirts of Mayfair, it took everything to withdraw his hand, push himself up from the settee, lock his hands behind his back, and stroll casually to the window.

He could not face her, of course. Further, he could not allow Willoughby to see how he'd been affected by thoughts of her—thoughts that, had she been Charles's wife and he discovered another man similarly contemplating her perfect imperfections, would have ended in that man's unconsciousness. Perhaps his death.

If she were mine, he thought, willing his erection to subside as he watched a hack rolling by beneath February's endless rain. *If she were mine, I would hide her away, keep her in the country, far from other men.*

Willoughby miscalculated his wife's potency. Understandable, he supposed. She did not resemble any siren he'd ever seen. His current mistress was far more beautiful, if one wished to be objective about it. But Julia Willoughby possessed a quality he'd rarely encountered. Never, in fact. She carried peace inside her.

Try as he might, he'd never tasted it. And he wanted to. He wanted to possess it.

He closed his eyes, picturing his mistress. That was no help, for Caro's face instantly transformed into a pair of dimples and smile-crinkled eyes. Gritting his teeth, he employed his only remaining weapon. A last resort.

He pictured his mother.

Immediately, his ardor began to cool.

Thanks be to God.

"Apologies for the delay, Wallingham." Boots tapped closer, muffling on the woolen carpet. "My wife ensures a household of such efficiency, I fear even papers I leave upon my desk are immediately filed in their proper place." Willoughby chuckled fondly.

The sound grated against Charles's spine like metal scraping stone. He held himself still, forced his jaw to unclench.

"For me, this means they are often lost, I fear. I do not share her organizational talents. However, I did manage to find the reports. One is from Essex. The others are from—"

"No need." Charles hadn't intended his voice to sound cold. It appeared to be one more failure of his control on this strange day. "You shall have my support."

As he turned, he saw Willoughby's pale brows arch above his spectacles. "I shall? Well, that is a fine piece of news—"

"Yes. Now I must depart, I'm afraid." He could not look directly at her, so he nodded vaguely in her direction. "Lady Willoughby, my thanks for the tea."

"Of course," she murmured. "It was my pleasure."

Pleasure. He loved hearing that word upon her lips.

He needed to leave. Something was wrong with him, clearly.

Uttering a simple "good day," he departed the Willoughbys' rented house on the outskirts of Mayfair. And prayed that his mistress could make him forget a certain married baroness who had turned tea, silence, and unexpectedly quickened breaths into the devil's own temptation.

Chapter Four

"Proper timing is a woefully underappreciated element of persuasion. Act too soon, and one risks being rebuffed. Too late, and one risks failure. Before breakfast, and one may be assured of the need for new employment."

—The Dowager Marchioness of Wallingham to her newest lady's maid in reply to an unsubtle solicitation for a day off.

One year and two months later – April 1817
Bedfordshire

It had been a year. Julia blinked down at the date she had written in her household journal: 13 April 1817. She could scarcely believe it. One year since she'd fled London in a panic she could not explain to herself, let alone Arthur. One year since she'd returned alone to Willoughby Manor, knowing she was a coward, but knowing nothing else for certain.

One year since she'd received the letter from her husband saying he would come home to Bedfordshire for Easter, and to expect him within a fortnight. One year since she'd stared into the coachman's bloodied, sodden countenance and read his grief there.

One year since Arthur had died on the road home, leaving her a widow rather than a wife. Leaving her alone.

She stroked a hand over the page, feeling the fine grain of the paper. Her journals had been his gift to her. He'd understood how dearly she loved keeping proper track of things, even though he did not understand why. Smiling softly, she thought of the way his hand would sometimes settle upon her shoulder. He'd never squeezed or rubbed. It was simply that: His hand, her shoulder. A spot of warmth and connection.

He'd been her husband, it was true. But he had also been her friend. Perhaps that most of all.

Her childhood had been a lonely one. Her father owned a bit of land outside Bedford, but no title and not a drop of aristocratic blood. And yet, her mother had pushed and prodded Julia to secure a titled husband. So much so that, by the time she was nineteen, she'd been desperate to escape. Desperate enough to take anyone.

Then, during a country dance one early September, she had caught Arthur's eye. She'd later marveled at her good fortune, for he was kinder than most gentlemen, warm and engaging and honest. She had worked tirelessly to be a proper wife to him, to make him proud. Perhaps she hadn't succeeded in all ways—her greatest failure was also her greatest heartbreak. Still, Arthur's love had shaped the woman she was for nine years.

Now, he was gone. Without him, she felt as blank as the page before her.

"Mrs. Willoughby to see ye, m'lady," came the voice of Julia's maid-of-all-work.

Julia glanced up from her desk. Peggy hovered uncertainly outside the doorway of Julia's small study. The dower cottage was tiny compared to Willoughby Manor, and the former chambermaid still had not accustomed herself to her change of duties—fewer rooms to clean, more time to spend answering calls and announcing guests. Simple enough, one would think.

Stifling a sigh, Julia nodded to the girl, whose fingers twisted at her waist. "Very good, Peggy. Please show her to the parlor and ask Cook to prepare a nice pot of tea. I shall join her shortly."

The girl nodded, her cap's frill bobbing along with her head as she turned on her heel and hurried to perform her assigned duties.

Carefully replacing her pen in the brass inkstand, Julia stood and smoothed the black crepe of her skirts over her hips, tugging at her sleeves to straighten them where they bunched inside the crooks of her elbows. The gown had not been fitted properly, as it had been made in haste mere days after Arthur's death, and although she had re-sewn the seams twice, her dissatisfaction remained.

A year, she thought. *Time for new gowns, I suppose. Gray, perhaps. Or lavender. I must remember to include it in next month's budget.*

She entered the parlor, smiling at the familiar form of Helen Willoughby. The dark-haired, sharp-nosed woman was in her mid-forties, but appeared ten years younger. Julia thought it was because her eyes always shone like those of a young girl eager for another piece of cake. Julia had come to adore her, which was just as well considering Helen was the mother of Arthur's cousin and heir, Miles. The new Lord Willoughby.

A year. Good heavens. Has it been so long?

Helen extended her hands, and Julia took them in her own, squeezing fondly.

"My dearest lady," Helen said, as she always did, tilting her head inquisitively. "How do you fare?"

For the first time, Julia felt a glimmer of resistance to the sympathy underlying her words. *I am a widow. It has been a year. How should I be? Perhaps you can tell me, for I cannot decide.* But these thoughts were peevish, so she instead answered as she had every day for the past six months: "I am well. And you?"

"Oh, you know," Helen released her fingers and waved dismissively as they each moved to their usual places on the rose-damask sofa. "Miles is chafing at the bit. It is enough to drive a mother mad." She described the young man's constant prattling about his imminent journey to London, where he would take his seat in the House of Lords for the first time. Apparently, the prospect of debating the laws of a kingdom worried him not at all, whereas the prospect of navigating the social complexities of the season and an admittedly perilous marriage mart had given the poor boy a megrim.

Peggy entered with the tea tray. Julia busied herself with pouring, taking care to fill Helen's cup only two-thirds full, as she preferred.

"Willoughby should not worry," she assured the older woman. "He is young and titled and handsome. If anything, I suspect *your* task will be the more arduous one, as you must ensure he chooses well from the many young ladies who will seek his favor."

Helen accepted the cup with a nod, but for a long moment, she did not glance up from where she cradled it in her hands. An additional oddity was her silence. Helen was rarely silent. Quite rarely. Julia could scarcely recall an occasion, in fact, other than this one.

Soon, however, she found herself wishing that silence had continued.

"That is what I ... oh, dash it all." Girlish, pleading eyes shot up to meet Julia's own. "You must come to London with us, I beg of you."

Julia could only blink. Her heart thundered at the mere thought. She could not return to London. Not as long as *he* was there.

"I know you deplore the city, my dear, and I realize you are still in mourning for our beloved Arthur, but I find myself dreadfully ill-prepared to guide Miles through his first season. Our acquaintances are few. I haven't the faintest clue what is required to gain entry to Almack's. Although, I have *heard* of Almack's. I suppose that is a mark in my favor. But how does Miles go about joining White's? Which invitations should one accept first? Which should be politely declined?" Her eyes widened comically. "Oh, dear. What if there are no invitations?"

Was Helen still speaking? Julia's limbs had frozen in place, her eyes riveted upon the other woman's teacup. All she could hear was the thud-and-swish of her pulse as it forced heated blood to the surface of her skin. That, and the word *London*.

He was bound to be there. A man of his influence could not miss a parliamentary session, surely.

"Utter disaster is likely, dear Julia. Utter. Disaster. I am certain of it."

"As am I," she murmured absently.

A feminine squeak pulled Julia's gaze up. "Then you will come?" Helen sat straighter, leaning forward and nearly spilling her tea. "Please say you will."

Julia shook her head and swallowed. "I—I cannot. I am sorry."

Gray-clad shoulders slumped, but only slightly. "Julia ..."

"I am still grieving, Helen." It was not precisely a lie. Her grief was real. It had become a part of her, a ribbon of black woven inside her fibers.

Helen transferred her teacup carefully to the oak side table before resting her hand upon on Julia's forearm. "Of course you are. But you will feel his loss more keenly than ever if you have nothing to occupy you."

"I have the cottage to look after. And the garden. My roses."

"Julia."

She did not want to meet Helen's eyes. She knew what she would see there. Pity. Sympathy. A kind of motherly scolding.

A gentle finger raised her chin. "Recall that I am a widow, too. So, when I say this, you must know it is only because you are as dear to me as my own sister. If I had a sister. Which I do not. But you are just that dear."

In spite of her trepidation, Julia released a chuckle.

Helen joined in, laughing at herself as she often did. Then she waved it away. "You cannot allow yourself to molder like some forgotten round of cheese."

Julia cringed at the comparison.

Helen forged ahead. "It is past time to discard the black crepe and bombazine. To venture outside these cottage walls. Miles and I never wanted you living here, in any case. We wanted you to remain at Willoughby Manor."

Shaking her head and squeezing Helen's fingers, Julia replied, "You know I could not have stayed. It would not have been right." Neither could she have borne it.

The day before the new Lord Willoughby and his mother had arrived, Julia had moved into the dower cottage. Then, she had returned to the manor for a last look around.

Nine years of work. Nine years of meticulous cleaning schedules and meal planning and maid hiring and morning tea with the mousy vicar and his shrewish wife. Nine years of arranging Arthur's library, straightening his desk, reminding him to don his coat before riding to Luton. Then, suddenly, he was gone. Her life's work had ended, becoming the property of some *future* Lady Willoughby.

No, the dower cottage was where she belonged. For now. Until the new Lady Willoughby came to claim her place inside Julia's exquisitely furnished nest. *Moldy cheese, indeed.*

"Come with us to London. We need you, and you need to leave here for a while. To see more than these walls, fine and polished though they are."

Not London. Anywhere but there. I cannot face him.

Helen neither heard nor heeded her inner thoughts. "It is early yet to begin thinking of remarriage."

Yes much, much too early.

"But you mustn't do what I did, Julia. You are still young and lovely. It may not seem so now, but in a year or two, perhaps—"

She closed her eyes. "Helen." The word was a plea for mercy.

Warm hands held hers tightly. "After Freddy died, I devoted myself to my son. Miles was all that mattered to me. Miles and my memories. It felt too much a betrayal to think of marrying again. So, instead, I remained a widow. Now, very soon, Miles will marry. I may be a grandmother. A mother. A mother-in-law. But I will be alone, Julia. They will be a family, and I will be alone."

Julia opened her eyes. Helen's shone with tears. Not of sympathy or pity, but of real regret. "You will have me," Julia whispered.

Helen smiled, a tear overflowing. "No, my dearest lady. I will do everything in my power to see that you do not follow me down this foolish path." She sniffed and swiped the tear away, then chuckled. "Now, you must pack quickly. We leave day after tomorrow."

"Helen, I have not said I will come." Everything in her resisted it. She could not face him. She could not.

"You must come. I cannot manage without you."

Julia shook her head, her heart rising up to choke her. Helen had been a friend to her when she'd needed one most desperately. She'd never asked a thing of Julia apart from the occasional cup of tea.

But Helen did not know Julia's secret. Her shame. No one knew.

Perhaps not even Wallingham.

It was her one hope—that the entire thing had been a fevered fancy caused by boredom or restlessness. That she'd simply imagined the moment in her drawing room when the mere brush of his fingers had set her afire. Certainly, he'd not *seemed* the sort to inspire lustful fantasies. He was quiet. Dignified. Serious. A man of deep intellect and impressive competence and unwavering honor. Prior to that moment, she'd enjoyed their conversations immensely. He listened better than most men, those intelligent green eyes lighting and deepening and flashing in harmony to her words.

She'd seen him only as the Marquess of Wallingham, a powerful man who could help her husband. A gentleman with a subtle sense of humor. A man she held in high regard, but not one who quickened her heart or made her flesh melt and ache.

All of which had changed that day a little over a year ago, when she had sat beside him inside thick, hot silence. Felt his finger stroke her thigh through layers of silk and muslin. Wanted him more than she'd ever wanted anything. Even her husband.

"Do you really wish to remain here?" Helen's wild shrug demonstrated her exasperation. "After Miles marries, I mean."

Did she? Once a new Lady Willoughby arrived, Julia would become a dowager, a burden upon the estate and upon this as-yet-unknown young lady attempting to establish a family and home of her own.

It would be wrong, she knew. Julia was not even a blood relation, although Miles and Helen had treated her as such from the beginning. She owed them better than to haunt the estate like a bothersome specter or, worse, Helen's vividly described moldering cheese.

"No," she murmured in answer to Helen's question. "I do not wish to remain here. But I cannot …" She swallowed hard. "I cannot think of remarriage just yet."

Squeezing Julia's shoulders, Helen smiled. "No, of course not. In London, however, you will have opportunities to assess many more eligible gentlemen than you will find lurking among the roses behind the dower cottage."

Julia chuckled, shaking her head. "Undeniably true," she conceded.

"That is all you must do. Entertain the possibilities. Perhaps purchase a few gowns in colors other than black. And help me avoid embarrassment whilst we find a good match for my son."

She wanted to help. It was the right and proper thing to ensure Miles married well and that he and Helen were well received during their first season. But could she muster the courage she had once lacked?

Her stomach quivered, went shaky and sick. Her flesh followed suit.

Courage. For Miles and Helen. For your own pride's sake. Have courage.

Again, she swallowed. Breathed slowly. Then nodded. "I will go with you."

Helen shouted in triumph and enfolded her in a breathless hug.

Meanwhile, Julia's mind busied itself with a singular prayer: *Please, God. Let him have forgotten me.*

THE MOMENT SHE ENTERED THE ROOM, HE KNEW. NOTHING had changed. Certainly not the unprecedented fascination she inspired in him. For a year, he had tried to forget. Tried to convince himself he had been struck by a peculiarity of mood, the strange and specific longing for tranquility, resulting in an arbitrary fixation upon a woman representing all that was graceful and feminine.

He'd argued the point thoroughly with himself, changed mistresses twice, tasked his housekeeper with learning to brew a proper pot of tea. He'd remained unsatisfied. But he'd had little choice. Julia Willoughby could not be his, for she was married to another man.

Except now she was not. She was, in fact, a widow.

A current ran through his body from the bones outward, both sharp and hot.

He was standing near a pianoforte amidst a smattering of Dunston's guests, debating with the earl about the merits of breeding for disposition rather than speed, when his eye caught upon her hair. Shades of blonde, both soft and bright, mingled with intriguing skeins of champagne. She wore it more intricately styled than the previous year—looping curls brushed her forehead and cheeks while plaited strands formed a delicate double band from crown to coil.

His breath caught at the sight of her neck—that long, white neck lovingly caressed by candlelight, the small mole that he'd noticed the last time he had seen her. When he'd been pierced by lust for a woman he could not have.

"... spirited female gives a far superior ride, I daresay. What value is speed if one must fire a bloody pistol to bestir the creature's interest?"

Charles let his eyes wander down to her bodice—sheer black silk dotted with jet beads and layered over a white underdress—and murmured a general sound of agreement.

"Further, now that you've promised me three of Ceres's mares, I shall test my theory forthwith."

"I promised you nothing of the sort, nor would I." Although his words were for Dunston, Charles kept his eyes fixed firmly upon her. That was where they wished to reside. Upon her skin and her hair.

She was thinner than the last time he'd seen her, the ridge of her collarbone more prominent, the hollows of her cheeks deeper. But her eyes were the same. Warm and crinkling as she greeted Dunston's mother.

"Fetching. Still in mourning, I take it. How long has it been?"

"A year."

"Hmm. Was she quite attached?"

He did not know her well enough to say. "Presumably."

"Too soon, then. You might test the waters with a bit of

pleasant conversation. A ride in the park, that sort of thing."

Charles turned a frown of confusion upon his dapper friend. Dunston always appeared slightly amused, as though he had a Shakespearean comedy running constantly inside his head, complete with droll witticisms and cynical commentary. Now, as the man sipped grotesquely sweet orgeat punch and winced at the flavor, he appeared to be laughing at Charles.

"Why?" Charles asked.

Dunston sighed. Then chuckled. Then shook his head. "You might be brilliant in many regards, but you are not very good at this, you know."

"Good at what?"

"Women."

Charles blinked, wondering when the conversation had turned to his deficiencies. He heard more than enough on that subject from his mother. "I have no need to be."

Dunston nodded toward Julia Willoughby. "You do if you wish to woo that one."

She was whispering something to a young man who resembled her late husband—obviously the new Lord Willoughby—and an older, dark-haired woman whose brown gown appeared a decade out of fashion.

"What makes you think—"

"Wallingham, I have never known your mind to wander when the topic is horses. The moment she appeared, not only did your mind leave the conversation, your eyes led the charge."

"Her husband was an acquaintance. That is all."

Snorting, Dunston shot a look of disgust down into his cup. "Vile stuff," he muttered. "Come. Accompany me while I fetch something more palatable. As it happens, we shall pass by the lovely Lady Willoughby. Perhaps you might inquire after her health."

Charles almost refused. He would have. But Dunston did not ask his permission, merely starting for the corner of the drawing room where the trio of Willoughbys conversed in whispers.

Against his better judgment, he followed the lean lord around a pair of perfumed fops and several blonde ladies cooing their approval of the vile punch to Dunston's sister. Too soon, he arrived, stopping at Dunston's side while the earl made the introductions.

It was difficult to tear his gaze away from her, but he managed for politeness' sake as he bowed to both Miles Willoughby and the young man's mother, Helen. When Willoughby attempted to introduce Julia, Charles noted the pink rising in her cheeks.

"We are acquainted," she murmured, her eyes lifting no higher than his chin. "Lord Wallingham. I trust you are well."

He'd not been prepared for her coolness. Perhaps he should have been. His behavior at their last meeting had bordered on insulting, assuming she'd been aware of its cause.

"Quite so, Lady Willoughby." He kept his voice low and gentle, as he would with a nervous mare. Clearly, she had sensed his peculiar fascination with her and found it unwelcome. "It is good to see you visiting London again."

Her lashes fluttered a bit, her color rising higher. Strange, that. He'd not said anything suggestive. Had he? Truthfully, being near her, seeing the fine column of her throat ripple and tense, he might have said anything, for he felt not the slightest bit in control.

"L-lord Willoughby has taken his seat in Parliament. I have accompanied him and Mrs. Willoughby to town for the season."

Well, that seemed fairly obvious. He frowned. "Yes, I—"

"However, as I am still in mourning, I fear my appearances will be limited. You understand, of course."

"Of co—"

"Should you contemplate invitations of any sort. Not that you would. You are not fond of entertainments, as I recall."

Was she calling him boring? He thought she was.

"In any event, I could not accept. It is simply not possible."

His head jerked at her preemptive rejection. Aside from

being rather blunt, it was what his mother would have dubbed "unforgivably rude." His mother was an expert in rudeness.

"Julia," the dark-haired Mrs. Willoughby murmured through clenched teeth. "I am certain Lord Wallingham understands the limitations of mourning. However, we would not wish to imply that a kindness extended to you or our family would be unwelcome, particularly from such an esteemed gentleman. Wouldn't you agree?"

She still had not met his eyes. Nor had hers crinkled at the corners, her peach lips downturned and tight. Her silence spoke rather loudly, he thought. She was offended by his attraction to her. Repulsed by it.

Perhaps she was right. Even he did not understand the thing, and he'd battled himself over it for more than a year.

"Lady Willoughby, be assured that I shall refrain from issuing invitations you might find onerous." He bowed politely. "My condolences for your loss."

Turning on his heel, he left the room. Left Dunston's house while waving off the earl's protests, promising to meet him and the Duke of Blackmore at White's the following morning. Then, he mounted his horse and, with greater fervency than necessary in a quiet Mayfair square, he urged the animal to a run.

The sooner he left her far behind, the better. Surely she would agree.

"You've gone mad. Perhaps the grief has made you so. But that is a poor excuse."

Helen's castigation was no worse than what Julia had said to herself.

"I have apologized," Julia said quietly, focusing on her stitching.

"To me. And to Miles. Not to the man you insulted."

She cringed to remember it. His voice—deep and mellow—had made her scalp tingle. Her eyes had yearned to explore his face, the long nose, the substantial chin, the probing green gaze that saw too much and followed her every breath. He'd made her blush at the mere sight of him, standing lean and tall. He'd brought everything she'd feared rushing back: The strange charge in the air between them, like the moment between lightning flash and thunderous boom. An aching suspense. A breathless heat. She had needed to shove at him, repel him so thoroughly that he would not notice her reaction.

How could he not notice? You were red as a radish.

She fancied the heat was still with her, staining her skin, even a day later. "I shall send a note," she murmured to the sleeve she was re-stitching for the third time.

"Don't bother. I have invited him here for dinner this evening."

Julia's needle stopped. Her head came up slowly. "You did not."

Helen tilted her chin, appearing every inch the vexed mama. "Wallingham is a marquess. His fortune and influence are vast, which you know very well after Arthur's efforts to court his favor. We need the connection. Besides, Miles could do with an older man's guidance. He lost his father much too early. I should have remarried, dash it all."

Older man? Wondering at Helen's unaccustomed sour mood, Julia frowned. "Wallingham is hardly Methuselah."

Helen raised dark brows. "I did not say he was."

"Many would consider him a man in his prime, I daresay."

A small smile lifted one side of Helen's thin mouth. "Really?"

Julia sniffed, letting her hands and her sewing settle in her lap. "That bit of silver at his temples is misleading. He is not yet forty. Further, I believe it lends him a distinguished air which suits him quite well and sets him apart from other gentlemen who are far less fit and capable than he."

"Do you, now?"

"Yes. He is an avid rider. Athletic, in fact. His horsemanship is renowned, and his stables are the finest in England, you know."

"Well," Helen replied with a bemused smile. "Then, you won't mind being seated next to him when he comes for dinner."

Blinking, Julia squeezed a handful of silk crepe. "I—I would rather you did not invite him."

The girlish twinkle had returned to her eyes. "And I would rather you had not insulted one of England's most powerful men, but it appears we must both resign ourselves to disappointment."

In the end, Julia did apologize to Wallingham for her rudeness. Indirectly.

She was seated beside him in the blue dining room of their rented house, letting the boisterous conversation of Miles and Helen fill the space, gathering her courage while taking miniscule nibbles of roasted beef and trying not to stare at Wallingham's hands. He had exceptionally long fingers, giving his hands a lean and elegant shape. Additionally, he used them in a knowing sort of fashion, as though the path of each finger were marked in advance so that his motions were both efficient and deliberate. Deft. Sensual. She fancied watching him manage a set of reins would give her the shivers. Not that she wanted the shivers. She did not. The shivers had only ever stirred trouble.

And yet, even watching him lift a forkful of overly salted meat to his lips had her shivering in her seat. Right there next to him.

It was tea in the drawing room all over again.

She set her own fork down beside her plate. "The beef is too salty," she murmured, her eyes upon his hand.

The hand went motionless, poised atop a white linen tablecloth, his thumb balancing a silver fork.

"I am sorry, my lord."

"For the beef?"

"And other things."

She thought she heard him draw a deep breath, but she only had courage enough to apologize, not enough to look at him directly.

"It is I who am sorry, Lady Willoughby, if I have ever done anything to give offense. Such was not my intention."

Swallowing, she moved her gaze further up his dark sleeve. Perhaps a few inches at a time would end with her finding her everlasting spine. "You have done nothing to offend me. The fault is mine. The past year has been ..."

"No need to explain."

"I was not keen on coming up to London. I fear my reactions have been irregular and too heavily influenced by sentiment."

"Stop."

At the single, hard word, her eyes flew to his as though he'd jerked her with a line. And, oh, there it was. That kind intelligence. Dark-lashed, green, and focused. Her heart flipped and squeezed.

"I have behaved appallingly," she whispered, her shame choking her. Shame for how she had spoken to him last evening, yes, but more because of what she'd felt for him. What she still felt for him.

"Stop," he repeated, his voice low. Intimate. "It is done. Regrets will benefit neither of us."

Within his words lay a separate truth, like a hidden thread woven underneath. He understood. He knew how she felt because he'd felt the same. She had often wondered as much, knowing he had touched her deliberately through her gown. Knowing he had shot up from the settee like a man burned by a torch. Knowing he had fled when Arthur returned, abruptly departing without glancing at her again.

He understood. Her guilt. Her need. He was the only other human who possibly could. Heart pounding, she let the awareness of him expand until it filled her up inside. Soothed and inflamed at once.

"How do I ... do we ..." She whispered the words, hoping he had answers when she did not.

"Come for a drive with me. Tomorrow. In the park."

She swallowed. "I am not ready."

"Please. It is a beginning only. An exploration."

What was the right thing? She could accept, and it would start them down a path that, considering all that had come before, might be forever tainted by a single moment of shameful longing, a betrayal of her husband, if only in her heart.

On the other hand, she could refuse. And for the rest of her life she would wonder whether she had rejected something precious simply because it had begun too soon.

"I don't know what to do."

"A drive is nothing," he argued, his voice a pulsing persuasion. "Conversation. A bit of air. A pleasant afternoon."

She found herself smiling at his characterization. "Nothing?"

His lips turned up to match her grin. "Well. Not nothing. But entirely without expectation. I am a patient man, Lady Willoughby. Above all things."

Before she could think better of it, she lowered her eyes to his hand, still poised beside his plate. "A drive. Nothing more than that."

"I shall come for you at two."

Her throat had gone dry.

Long fingers. Long, long fingers.

She reached for her wine. Unable to speak, she drank deeply and nodded her assent.

Only a drive, Julia. An hour exchanging inane pleasantries. Time enough to realize he is only a man like many others. Then, perhaps you may break free of his peculiar spell.

Chapter Five

"You may wish to alter your courtship techniques, Charles. A lady only has so many bonnets, you know."

—The Dowager Marchioness of Wallingham to her son, Charles, upon learning the deleterious effect of sudden downpours upon a certain widow's disposition.

∞

For a disaster, their outing began auspiciously enough. He came for her precisely at two, arriving in his recently purchased barouche. And, he noted, she was gowned not in black but in a white muslin gown and dark-gray velvet spencer. Her bonnet was covered in black silk, but she appeared to be exiting full mourning for the paler shades of half mourning.

A promising sign, that.

Warmth uncoiled in his chest at the sight of her. His heart leapt and surged as she placed her white-gloved hand in his, stepping up into the open carriage.

Of course, she was quiet and visibly vibrating with nerves.

Thinking it would set her at ease, he began with a neutral—if not particularly invigorating—topic as the coachman drove them west toward Hyde Park. "The carriage is new," he murmured, wishing he had something to do with his hands other than rest them on his thighs. His palms itched inside his gloves. "It has a movable axle, which prevents oversetting and allows the vehicle to turn more easily in a smaller space."

"Mmm. The design is lighter and less cumbersome for the horses as well, is it not?"

His eyes flared and flashed to her face. "You are familiar with movable axles?"

She blinked, her eyes darting away as pink bloomed in her cheeks. "Only what I have read. I am certain your expertise on the subject is superior."

"Why are you certain of that?"

She looked as though she wanted to squirm but was stifling the urge with all her might. "Gentlemen have an interest in such things."

"As do you, evidently."

Her lips pressed together as though she wished to say something. Instead, she remained silent and kept her eyes trained on the passing street.

He took the opportunity to study her, puzzled once again by his own enchantment. Her face was pretty, though hardly exceptional. Her voice was soft and gentle, her lips curving and pursing with subtlety rather than emphasis, more soothing than seductive. Before her husband's death, her manner had been charmingly polite, but no more so than many titled wives and matrons. Now, he noted, the polished veneer had worn thin in places, exposing glimpses of dark grief, bright streaks of tense uncertainty.

A fat, wet drop splashed onto her sleeve, beading on the velvet. Glancing up, he saw the clouds he'd presumed would pass without incident instead gathering into plump billows.

He frowned. "I fear our outing may be short-lived."

"I knew I should not have said anything." Though her words were muttered under her breath, he heard every one. He could not help it. His senses were locked upon her in a way that was both automatic and a trifle worrisome.

"About what?"

Finally, she turned toward him. Her cheeks remained pink, but her eyes had lost their frantic light. Now she appeared ... disappointed. "The patented axle." Her fingers laced and unlaced in her lap. "It was poor judgment on my part. I shall understand if you would prefer to take me home."

What in blazes was she on about? He could not decide where he had lost the thread of the conversation. Several times, he opened his mouth to inquire, only to stop and search his memory for clues. He'd mentioned the carriage. She had seemed knowledgeable. The rain had started. He'd commented that their ride might prove abbreviated because of poor weather.

No, he would have to ask. "Forgive me, Lady Willoughby, but what in blazes are you on about?"

Her shoulders stiffened. "You needn't speak to me in such a way."

"I did beg your forgiveness."

"Yes, but you did not mean it."

"I have entirely lost track of our conversation."

She sniffed. "That is no cause for rudeness."

Momentarily stymied, he attempted to regain his footing. "I apologize."

Silence.

"What did you mean when you said you should not have spoken about the axle?"

Another sniff. "It is a subject for gentlemen. Not ladies."

"The axle?"

"Yes. Ladies should have no interest in such matters."

He could not unfrown, could not look away from this odd, black-bonneted creature beside him. "Whyever not?"

"It is unfeminine to be overly learned in subjects better understood by gentlemen. Worse still to presume to discuss them knowledgeably." She spoke this nonsense with assurance. Authority, even.

Nothing for it. He was flummoxed. "Where did you hear this?"

Her chin tilted. "It is well understood, my lord. In the third edition of *The Pleasing Companion: A Female's Complete Guide to Admirable Comportment and Domestic Economy*, the author, Mr. Crane, recommends avoiding masculine subjects, as a lady may either expose her ignorance or give insult through unseemly expertise."

It took several seconds for him to respond. "Pure rubbish."

"Mr. Crane does not think so."

"Then, Mr. Crane is rubbish. Aside from which, you have no need to consult manuals on feminine comportment. You are the very definition of admirable. You should speak of those things that interest you. Nothing more, nothing less."

Two drops landed upon her chin as she tilted her head up to stare at him.

Without thinking, he gently wiped them away with his thumb. It was a bold maneuver, and he wished he could say it had been deliberate. But it wasn't. From the beginning of their acquaintance, he had felt vaguely proprietary with her, as though he'd known her for years, and their relationship was one of familiar affection.

She blinked slowly, her lips parting. "Perhaps we should raise the canopy, my lord."

He swallowed. Withdrew his hand. Called out instructions to his coachman to proceed to the park before stopping to make the adjustment.

Then, he cleared his throat. Studied his glove as though it held the pedigree of a new, blooded champion. They sat in silence for long minutes, the only sounds those of the street—hooves and wheels, whicker and creak. Leaves and wind, shuffle and sigh. More distant were the shouts and laughter of two coal men, the shriek of an irate woman selling milk.

"I ..." She stopped, nibbling her lower lip. "I suppose if you do not find it objectionable, we might converse about the new axle design."

By this point, he noted she was rosy pink from bonnet brim to dainty chin. What manner of woman was abashed to discuss carriages? Most puzzling. "If it interests you, Lady Willoughby, I shall happily discuss it. However, I am curious as to your reliance upon the advice of Mr. Crane. To my recollection, you had no need of such guidance."

The rain had begun a soft patter upon the street and the wool of his coat. She cast an uneasy glance skyward before replying, "I enjoy books of the sort Mr. Crane writes."

His frown deepened. "Surely they are intended for young women. Ladies newly married or seeking a match. That sort of thing."

She turned her gaze slowly upon him, the brown now snapping with offense.

Bloody hell. He'd let his curiosity rule his mouth, and now he'd managed to call her old. "I did not mean to imply—"

Her lips pursed, the corners flattening. "One should always strive to better one's knowledge and skills, whether one is a new bride or an ancient widow."

Blast. Lemons were sweeter than her tone. "You are not ancient. That is not what I—"

"How you flatter me, my lord." Peach lips were puckered and tight. Her shoulders were rigid. And now she refused to look at him.

Bloody hell. "I apologize."

The rain fell steadily now, pattering in the silence, answering him with disdain. Finally, they reached the park. Charles climbed down and busied himself helping the coachman raise the canopy.

Except that it would not budge.

"M'lord, it appears this hinge is stuck," the coachman observed, eyeing the increasing rain, now accompanied by brisk wind that had Lady Willoughby rubbing her upper arms. "Shall I attempt to force it?"

The man asked because, as he knew, wrenching the hinge would likely damage the rather expensive new carriage. Charles glanced toward the woman whose black bonnet and white skirts were being slowly dampened. He sighed. Then looked at John Coachman across the width of said carriage and nodded regretfully.

A loud crack, then the groan of malfunctioning metal sounded as he and the coachman dragged the canopy upward. He tried to snap it into place. It refused to hold, one side of the retractable structure sagging woefully.

Bloody hell. He met the coachman's consternation with a grim stare.

"I—I am trying, m'lord."

The thing collapsed and sagged, the broken hinge lacking the tension to hold it erect.

Lady Willoughby's frowning face poked around the edge of the canopy. "Your carriage appears to be in some disrepair, my lord."

"Yes," he gritted. "So it does."

She sniffed. "Perhaps we should return home before—"

"We are not bloody well returning home."

Her head jerked upright before retreating behind the half-raised half-top.

"I apologize." The words ground out of him. He was not typically a surly sort, but this outing was growing worse moment by moment. And he had no one to blame but himself. "John," he called across the bloody malfunctioning carriage.

"Aye, m'lord."

"Secure it as best you can. Then drive us along Rotten Row for a bit. Should the rain increase, return to Lady Willoughby's residence at once."

By the time they had gone a hundred yards, the rain had become a downpour. Lady Willoughby's skirts lay sodden over her knees, her lips a cool and bitter pinch, the silence thick as spoiled custard in the growing gloom.

And that was before the bloody canopy again collapsed backward on a sudden gust.

"Oh!" she cried, her hands flying up as a blast of rain—now nearly solid and sheeting sideways—struck their faces.

"Bloody hell." The words cracked from his own mouth, barking without his permission.

"Lord Wallingham!" she protested.

"I apologize." How many did that make? Four? "John! Stop the carriage and fix this bloody thing."

The man did stop, but the rain did not. Charles eyed his companion. She was now utterly drenched, her gown a sodden mess, her bonnet a poor protection. Glancing around, he spied a tree roughly twenty feet away, beneath which they might escape the better part of the rain's wrath.

"Come," he said, climbing down and offering her his hand.

She stared at him, eyes wide, lashes dripping. Every inch of her skin was wet. And she was not moving, her posture rigid and tense. "I would prefer to go home."

Her tone was crystalline frost. He nearly flinched. Instead, he gritted his teeth. "While John Coachman repairs the top, we may shelter beneath that tree." He nodded toward the largest one along this stretch of the Row. "Then I shall take you home."

She squinted at the tree, then at him, then down at her skirts before sighing and placing her hand in his. Attempting to climb down from the carriage while hampered by wet, clinging muslin, Lady Willoughby huffed a bit, grunting as her foot slipped on the step and her knees failed to accommodate the new position of her lower legs, pitching her forward.

Into his arms.

He found himself holding her awkwardly, her soft, ample, wet-velvet-covered bosom abruptly plastering itself to his face.

She squawked.

He attempted to stabilize her, clutching and grasping what he could. As it happened, "what he could" was her backside.

She screeched.

He lifted and lowered her instantly to the ground. Her desperate, clawing hands sent his hat flying and yanked painfully at his hair on the way down. To avoid being separated from his scalp, he stooped and uncurled her fingers gently, then drew a much-needed breath and opened his eyes.

"I apologize," he said for the fifth time.

Oh, God. She was livid. Soaked and dripping and red and bloody furious.

In the interest of averting an explosion, he didn't bother to ask permission. He simply grasped her hand and tugged her toward the tree. Dimly, he realized he was dragging her behind him as he heard her protesting gasp.

"Wallingham!"

He moved faster. Gripped her hand harder. Finally, they reached the dubious shelter of the tree's dripping, leafy boughs. He turned his back to the trunk and tugged her beside him onto the raised ground around its base.

Her bonnet brim dripped. Her rounded lips gleamed. Her bosom heaved on furious breaths. Brown eyes blazed with aggravation.

But she was no longer being soaked by the equally furious downpour. Which was the point.

"This is outrageous," she sputtered. "I am not an infant to be jerked about by leading strings."

"I apologize."

Her outrage maintained its bristle. "You keep saying that, but you are obviously not sorry at all."

He glanced upward. "I should think you would be grateful for my swift action."

"Grateful? Look at me! I am a mess. My gown is ruined. My bonnet will never be the same—"

"I shall replace them."

"It is highly improper to even suggest it."

He ground his teeth, sighing in exasperation. "What would you have me do?"

"Take me home."

Narrowing his eyes upon her, he replied, "You agreed to a drive."

"My error, clearly."

"Am I to blame for the weather?"

Her well-defined jaw flexed. "You have turned unfortunate circumstances to your advantage, taking great ... liberties with my person."

He raised his brows. Liberties? She had no idea how restrained he had been. But it was time to inform her. He moved closer, lowering his head near hers. "Have I kissed you, Lady Willoughby?"

She blinked four times, droplets flying from her eyelashes. Her lips parted on an O.

"Have I?" he demanded, his voice low and hard with his frustration.

Those damp lips firmed as she swallowed. "No."

"But I have wanted to. I want far more than kisses. More than you can imagine." He let his eyes drop to her bodice, where gray velvet could not disguise the lushness of her body's curves. "Whatever liberties you suppose I have taken thus far, they are nothing compared to my desires."

The bodice swelled on her next breath then fell on a sigh. "We cannot." It was scarcely a whisper, but he heard. *We*, she had said. *We*. Not *you*.

His eyes came up to hers. And there it was. A desire to match his own. "What is to stop us?"

"This is wrong."

"You are no longer married."

"It has only been a year."

"I have wanted you for longer."

She looked away, her brow descending in displeasure. "That is why it is wrong."

"Because I wanted you before—"

Her gaze slammed back into his with heart-seizing force. "No. Because *I* wanted *you.*" Her lower lip trembled then firmed. "I loved my husband. Ours was a good marriage. What I felt for you was a betrayal of my vows. Of him."

Seeing her distress twisted something inside him, the pain sharp and biting between his chest and stomach. He inched closer, wanting to shelter her. "Feelings are not betrayal, Julia. Had we acted upon them while you were his wife, perhaps you would be right. But we did not."

Her eyes closed. She swayed toward him.

Gently, he slid his hands beneath her elbows, not daring to do more here in Hyde Park. The sheeting rain and shadows of the tree might give them some protection, but they were only a few dozen yards from the curious gaze of the beau monde.

"Let us begin again," he said softly, the constant sigh of rain surrounding them in a kind of intimacy. "No past. No demands. Simply a man who admires a woman and wishes to spend time with her."

Her eyes opened, amontillado sherry that both intoxicated and drowned a man. "I am not seeking a mere liaison. If we continue, it must be with that understanding."

He froze. Marriage. She wanted marriage. At one level, he admired her honesty. But he had resisted marrying again for so long, a part of him cringed at the notion. Memories of his first marriage fortified his determination in that regard.

As he stared down at Julia Willoughby, however, a greater vision swamped those dim recollections. A vision of her pouring a perfect cup of tea as sunlight caressed her neck. A vision of her stroking his cheek and smiling up at him with familiar affection. A vision of her lying beside him. Beneath him. Atop him. All around him. For the rest of his life.

More than he wanted a night or two—even a month or two—he realized he wanted a lifetime with her. Which meant marriage.

"I understand," he answered hoarsely.

She tilted her head. Caught her breath with him. Let the moment swell as they both realized what had been said.

This would end in marriage.

Whatever occurred between now and that moment—the moment she became his—constituted only details. He could be patient. He could wait for her.

Finally, she nodded her acceptance. "Good," she murmured.

Slowly, he smiled, liking her answer. Liking the rain. Liking the thought that all he must do is wait, and she would belong to him. Liking that her fate was sealed as surely as his was. "Good, indeed."

Chapter Six

"Patience? At this rate, I shall sooner attend my funeral than my son's nuptials."

—The Dowager Marchioness of Wallingham to Lady Berne upon said lady's enviable news of expectant grandmotherhood.

∞

One year and seven months later – November 30, 1818
Fairfield Park, Suffolk

He'd waited long enough, Charles decided as he listened to Dunston natter on about the stakes at Newmarket. Perhaps he'd given a damn about Thoroughbreds and winnings seven months ago. Today, the only topic that interested him was Julia. More specifically, giving her a new title—the

Marchioness of Wallingham. And a new place to sleep—in his bed.

Of course, this goal required a better plan than the one he'd employed for the past two years. Wooing her in a conventional manner with such niceties as carriage rides and quadrilles had failed rather miserably. He'd wished to convey proper respect by demonstrating he could control his lust, showing her it was merely one reason of many why he wanted to make her his wife.

Instead, his *caution* had allowed her to escape his grasp.

And so the niceties would end. Because they must. Because he could not allow her to marry Sir Mortimer bloody Spalding, the gray-haired widower she had deemed a suitable husband.

He shot a glare in the baronet's direction and took a sip of cognac. As usual, the man looked as though he'd been caught in a windstorm after falling from a hayloft. God knew what Julia found so bloody *suitable*.

"I understand your mother arrived at Steadwick this morning. An unusual occurrence, no?"

Returning his gaze to Dunston, Charles snorted before nodding. "Stunned the devil out of me. She never travels this time of year."

"What do you suppose prompted it?"

He glanced at Julia across the drawing room. She sat with her usual composed demeanor beside Willoughby's mother, Helen, nibbling a biscuit and taking occasional sips of tea. Dressed in a long-sleeved gown of rose velvet, she kept her eyes downcast, avoiding looking his way.

"I have my suspicions," he murmured. "But Mother insists she simply wished to spend Christmastide with her sole offspring."

Dunston frowned. "When was the last time—"

"Fourteen years ago."

"Ah. Some other reason, then."

"Very likely."

In fact, his mother had all but confirmed his suspicions

when she had oh-so-casually inquired whether he had spoken to "a certain widow" recently, as she'd been given to understand Lord Dunston had stooped to populating his annual hunt with Whig rabble.

Rather than answering, he had invited her to commandeer whatever bedchamber she liked, so long as she did not give his servants cause to poison her soup.

She had arched a single white brow above a familiar glare. "Mind your tongue, boy," she'd snapped. "Kindly answer my question."

He'd studied his mother's face and replied, "I have seen her."

"And?"

Looking down into eyes that were a mirror of his, he'd been puzzled by the shadows there. His mother was worried. His mother *never* worried. Just like she never traveled after September.

"All is well," he'd said quietly, seeking to soothe what appeared to be concern for him. She was his mother, after all, and she loved him with a mother's fervent intensity. He loved her in return, despite their many battles and her constant attempts to bend him to her will.

She'd responded to his reassurance with a sniff of disdain, but he'd been glad to see the tension around her mouth ease. "I am gratified you have come to your senses at last," she'd said crisply. "For a clever boy, you are remarkably dense in your infatuation with that creature."

Having little desire to relive the same argument yet again, he had simply kissed her wrinkled cheek and instructed his housekeeper to prepare a light luncheon for the dowager marchioness. Then, eager to be elsewhere, he had departed for Fairfield.

Presently, he stood listening to Dunston reminisce about Lady Wallingham's more amusing eccentricities, including her demand the previous year that the earl supply her with one of his prime scent hounds, a pup she had subsequently named

Humphrey. Naturally, this had come a mere month after she'd declared all dogs a costly menace useful only for the defilement of carpets and slippers. Dunston had been surprised by her change of heart. Charles had not.

"Do you suppose I should invite her to dine with us?" Dunston mused. "She does add a certain something to one's table."

Charles sipped his cognac and resumed his examination of Julia's gown. In particular, her bodice. In greater particular, her neckline, which was squared and trimmed with brown ribbon. He thought it rather flattering to the roundness of her breasts.

Perhaps tonight he would finally discover whether those breasts were tipped with peach or some other color.

Yes. He nearly smiled at the thought. Tonight, the wondering would end and the real courtship of Julia Willoughby would begin.

JULIA'S STOMACH HAD BEEN A BURNING KNOT FOR TWO DAYS. Even the satisfaction of bringing sanity to Lord Dunston's library had done little to ease it. Now, she bit into a dry, crumbly biscuit and tried not to stare at the reason for her distress.

He stood a dozen feet away, across the Fairfield drawing room. Tall and dark and impeccable, his profile was that of an aristocrat, his eyes those of a conqueror. Perhaps it was just her fancy. Others seemed not to notice. She'd seen it too often to ignore the implications. The man was relentless—patient but relentless.

Beside her, Helen clicked her tongue. "Will you look at that? It's dangling again."

At Julia's querying glance, Helen nodded toward the window, where Sir Mortimer Spalding stood in animated conversation with Miles. The man's peppery gray hair was in disarray, the shoulder seam of his riding coat sporting several loosened threads—in other words, he looked the same as he always did.

I really should make a greater effort to speak with him, she thought dully, realizing she'd done so only once since arriving at Fairfield. *He is the reason why I attended this hunt, after all. Isn't he?*

"I should think his fondness for his dratted quizzing glass would cause him to take greater care." Of late, Helen often expressed criticism for Sir Mortimer. In fact, she'd paid far more attention to the disheveled-but-comfortingly-pleasant widower than Julia had done over the past several months, conversing at length about obscure botanical matters and arguing about Sir Mortimer's "incompetent" valet. The two had known one other since childhood, having grown up in the same village near Cambridge, so their familiarity was not surprising. But over time, Helen's tone had become sharper, more ... proprietary, as it was now.

"When you are his wife, I do hope you will insist he make better use of pockets. For a man of his age to go about with his chain swinging free is positively undignified." Helen's nose wrinkled as she took a sip of tea.

When you are his wife.

Biscuit crumbs lumped inside Julia's throat. She swallowed hard, but they would not go down. Compulsively, her gaze found Charlie.

And collided with glittering, purposeful green.

A cheerful giggle came from the girl on the opposite side of Helen. "Doubtless she will stitch the chain into place, Mama. Julia has no tolerance for disorder." The girl—yellow-haired and blue-eyed, more pretty than bright—leaned forward to shoot a merry, mischievous grin at Julia.

Knowing she must answer, Julia played along, arching a falsely reproving brow at Miles Willoughby's new, young bride. "I noticed you left your copy of Mr. Crane's *The Pleasing Companion* on the parlor settee, Olive. Perhaps you should master a subject before you dismiss it willy-nilly."

"Oh, pooh." Olive waved and laughed. "I read three chapters, I'll have you know. Mr. Crane is nothing but a fusty old scold."

Julia grinned and shook her head before retrieving her tea from a gilded tray. She wished she could relax into her usual banter with Olive—the girl had staunchly resisted Julia's efforts to instruct her in proper household management, but with such unflinching good humor, Julia had never been able to take offense. Instead, the differences in style between herself and the new Lady Willoughby emphasized how little Julia was needed at Willoughby Manor. Both Miles and Olive had shown her great kindness, and Helen was Julia's dearest friend, but it was clearly time to move on. To do that, she must marry.

Again, her eyes strayed to Charlie.

With a slow, grinding effort, she dragged her gaze away, staring down into brown liquid and wondering when this hideous, hollow ache would stop.

Murmurs erupted near the entrance where Lord Dunston's sister, Lady Stickley, stood with her husband and two blonde companions.

Helen craned her neck up and forward and side to side. "Who do you suppose ...?" Her murmured question was soon answered as a purple plume bobbed past Lord and Lady Stickley's twin expressions of alarm. The feather was attached to a velvet turban.

Which was, in turn, crowning the white coiffure of a tiny, birdlike woman radiating the hauteur of a queen.

"Dunston!" the queen bellowed in her outsized, trumpeting voice. "It appears your note inviting me to supper has been waylaid. Perhaps you should inquire as to its whereabouts."

Having halted mid-conversation with Charlie, the handsome, affable Lord Dunston closed his mouth, raised a wry brow, and quirked his lips before crossing the room to greet the lady demanding his attention. He bowed to her politely, yet with a certain mocking wit.

Julia had not suspected a man's posture could contain wit, but apparently, Dunston's could.

"My dear lady," he purred. "I should be most distraught to learn my note went astray. Had I sent one."

Her response was an imperious sniff, her purple feather a bobbing courtier. "That explains it. I assumed your mother instilled better manners in her only son. I assumed wrong."

Dunston merely grinned with insouciant charm. "Alas, I was unaware of your arrival at Steadwick Park until this very hour, my lady. Do join us. I was just conveying to Lord Wallingham the need for additional grandeur at my table."

She tapped his upper arm with her folded fan. "Curb your cheek. I am no simpering miss to be assuaged by a fine waistcoat and a charming grin."

He glanced down admiringly at the silver silk, giving the embroidered edge an appreciative stroke. "It is rather fine, is it not?" He offered her his arm. "A Frenchman's work, of course. They are wretched for conversation, but one cannot deny their utility with a needle."

The old woman, garbed from turban to slippers in purple velvet, released a snort and gave him another whack with her fan before taking his elbow. "If one can abide poor hygiene and detestable character, one supposes they have their uses. Seamstress. Cook. Cannon fodder."

Dunston laughed in his rich, mellow way and escorted her the length of the room to the dark-haired man with glittering green eyes.

Eyes a perfect match for hers.

"Mother," Charlie said. "How ... unexpected."

Their voices lowered to grim utterances until Julia could

only make out every fourth or fifth word. Which was odd, given that Dorothea Bainbridge, the Dowager Marchioness of Wallingham, routinely out-bellowed women twice her size. In certain circles, she was regarded as a dragon, fierce and opinionated and blunt. Certainly, her influence was disproportionately weighty both inside and outside London.

But to Julia, she was the woman who had birthed Charlie. Raised him to be the strong, noble, brilliant man he was. True, Lady Wallingham had long rankled her son with her manipulations, infuriated him with her meddling, irritated him with her relentless pontificating and endless criticisms. She had also loved him, protected him. In many ways—perhaps most ways—Julia looked upon Lady Wallingham with something like gratitude, if not outright admiration.

But there was more than one side to the dragon, as Julia had discovered.

"What are they saying?" Helen hissed into Julia's ear.

Julia shook her head and answered in a murmur, "I had no idea she would be here. She never leaves Northumberland this time of year."

Dash it all. She was rhyming again. A sure sign of distress.

"Julia?"

She watched Charlie's expression, eyes darkening, jaw tight, neck stiff. That mouth she so adored flattened into a line of displeasure. Then his eyes moved over his mother's shoulder.

Landed upon Julia.

And she was washed in heat. Then cold. Then heat again.

"Are you all right, dear?" It was Helen.

No, she was not.

"Is your stomach paining you?"

Julia shook her head and swallowed, her mouth dry and sticky despite the tea. Finally, she closed her eyes and severed their connection. Glanced down and saw her hand had drifted again. Forced her fingers to unclench and move from her belly to her lap.

"I must go," she whispered, studying the lines of her knuckles. The pointy bones and rounded nails and slender wrist of her own hand.

Another hand came to cover hers. Helen again. "Then go. I shall make your excuses to Lord Dunston and Sir Mortimer."

Without another thought, or even glancing up, Julia set her tea neatly on the tray before her, patted Helen's hand in thanks, and fled past Lord Dunston's sister, out of Lord Dunston's drawing room, down Lord Dunston's corridor and stairs. She did not know where she was going, for there was nowhere she belonged.

As it happened, she passed Peggy outside the dining room and asked her to fetch her cloak. Then, Julia stood like a ninny there in the empty, oak-paneled dining room, clutching her own waist and struggling to breathe.

It was too much. Seeing him. Seeing his mother.

The last time she had spoken to Lady Wallingham, the woman had summoned her to Wallingham House on Park Lane. There, in a bright-yellow parlor decorated with rose-hued velvets and portraits of richly gowned women, Charlie's mother had served tea and surprisingly buttery biscuits while slowly, ruthlessly forcing her to break her own heart.

She'd been elated to receive the dowager's note, since Charlie had declared his affections only the week before, proclaiming that she must consent to be his wife because he could not go much longer without taking her fully. Of course, he'd had his hand working beneath her skirts and his lips nibbling from her mouth to her breast at the time, so she had taken his declarations with a touch of skepticism. Her heart had not. It had leapt and pounded a deafening drumbeat of celebration.

Their courtship had never been easy, and after numerous mishaps and more than one ruined hat, Julia had nearly convinced herself to set all her misgivings aside—to forget about their imperfect beginning and odd, stumbling, chaotic middle—

and focus on how he made her feel. Which was glorious. Hot and flushed and out of control. Sensual and womanly and so dashed *grateful* to be near him, she could scarcely breathe.

If their ending could be that, then she would happily forget everything else, she'd reasoned. On the verge of consenting to become his wife, she had not thought twice when Lady Wallingham's note arrived. She'd met her future mother-in-law for tea, determined to befriend the dragon.

And the dragon had calmly, quietly explained that Charles could not possibly marry someone like her. That to even contemplate it was proof that Julia did not love him.

For, what kind of woman consigns the man she loves to live out his days with no hope of fathering children?

Yes, the dragon was blunt. And ruthless.

And right.

"Your cloak, m'lady." The brown wool appeared under her nose. A drop fell onto its surface.

Julia quickly swiped her cheek with a bony knuckle and tossed the thing over her shoulders. "Thank you, Peggy." She whispered the words. Or perhaps she only thought them. Speaking was difficult now.

Head down, she made for the main entrance hall. Nodded to the butler as he swept open ten-foot oak doors, then charged out into the stunning chill.

Her slippers skated a bit as she took the four steps down to the drive. Everything was crystalline with frost—bare branches, shorn grass, stone walls. The world was a frozen realm of gray and white.

She did not know where she was going. But it didn't matter.

Two heartbeats passed as her breath roiled and steamed before her.

Deliberately, she drew her cloak tighter and continued walking. One step. Two steps.

Breathing. One breath. Two breaths.

Beating. One beat. Two beats.

This was all she had left. All she knew to do—go forward into a frozen landscape and hope eventually the pain would ease.

Chapter Seven

"If you are opposed to such 'manipulations,' I recommend giving me what I want. A mother's desire to intervene is directly proportionate to the incompetence of one's offspring."

—The Dowager Marchioness of Wallingham to her son, Charles, regarding the source of false and pernicious rumors about a certain widow.

∞

He found her in the stables, of all places, rearranging the harnesses on their pegs according to size. Stopping just inside the entrance, he waited and watched. She bent to gather two buckets, one of which had toppled onto its side and rolled several feet away. It was returned neatly to a spot precisely in the center of a row of hanging bridles. On either side, she placed a smaller bucket.

She had explained it once, how putting everything in its proper place calmed and soothed her mind. Even her peculiar habit of unintentional rhyming, she had confessed, was a manifestation of her need for symmetry.

The oddity made him smile every time.

He let his eyes explore. Devour. Wisps of blonde hair floated away from their confines, brushing her cheeks and flirting with light from the stable window. The tip of her nose was red, her breath white, her cloak brown. She moved gracefully, efficiently, pausing here and there to examine her work.

"Is it color or length?" he asked, moving slowly, deliberately deeper into the dim interior.

Her back stiffened, her fingers fluttering at her sides. She wore no gloves. "Length," she answered without turning. She tugged one bridle a fraction of an inch before finally facing him. "What are you doing here, Charlie?"

She was the only one who had ever called him Charlie. To his mother, he was Charles or "boy." To his friends, he was Wallingham. But during their first kiss, Julia had panted and melted and turned him inside out before groaning, "Oh, Charlie. Again, my darling." Perhaps it had been the best rhyme she could muster in the moment, or perhaps she liked the sound of it, but she had spoken his name the same way ever since. He craved hearing it upon her lips with a consuming need.

Now, he moved toward her, answering, "You know."

Those sherry eyes sheened and gleamed unexpectedly before squeezing closed.

His heart twisted. He rushed forward, wrapping her in his arms.

She whimpered, her forehead dropping against his shoulder. "I cannot bear this." Her desperate whisper knifed his gut.

Clutching her tighter, he cradled her precious head against him and laid his lips beside her ear. "I'll do anything to stop you hurting, Julia. Anything."

"You must let me go," she sobbed.

"Except that."

She gave a wet chuckle and wrapped her arms around his waist, fisting the wool at his back. "Driving me mad," she growled, the feminine ferocity causing him to grin like a fool. "You are driving me mad."

He nuzzled and nibbled her neck, loving the feel of her arms, the rosy scent of her skin. "Only because you deny us both what we need."

She shoved away from him, backing up with one arm extended like a shield. Wet streaks gleamed upon her face. "We cannot be together."

"Nonsense."

"I intend to marry Sir Mortimer."

A dark, furious chill stiffened his spine. "Ah. And when is the wedding?"

"Do not mock me." Her indignant, narrow-eyed response sent a thrill of satisfaction through him.

"So, this 'understanding' is more yours than his. Interesting."

"We suit. It is only a matter of time before he sees it. He is a kindly man in need of a wife. I am a widow in need of a husband."

"Mmm. Only one problem with your perfect symmetry, love." Remarkably, he managed to keep his voice steady and low. He wanted to shout. To roar. But a lifetime of disciplining his responses served him well. "You. Are. Taken."

She turned to pace toward an empty stall, repositioning the gate so it was open fully. Her agitation was obvious, even before he saw the trembling in her hands.

He closed in upon her, herding her inside the stall. She stumbled back, again raising a staying hand.

"Charlie, please."

He advanced on her until her hand flattened on his chest. Until her back reached the brick wall. Until there was nothing between them but a few layers of wool and their heat, their breath.

"I—I cannot marry you."

"Of course you can," he snapped. "This is nothing but bloody foolishness."

"No."

"You want me." He cupped her face, drawing her beautiful jaw forward, forcing her eyes to meet his. "Just as I want you."

Her brow crumpled. "Want." She swallowed hard. "Yes. But that is not ... love."

The pain of her statement nearly bent him in half. It gouged and tore at his insides. Infuriated and incited his baser instincts.

He'd felt similar agony last spring on Rotten Row. Seated beside her in his best phaeton, he'd listened to her methodically list all the reasons why she could not marry him. After two years of careful courtship and numerous signals of affection and infatuation—she'd come within a hairsbreadth of letting him bed her only two days earlier—he'd been so stunned by her about-face, the reins had slipped from his hands. The horses had spooked. The carriage had careened out of control. They'd been saved by the quick actions of two good men, Lord Tannenbrook and Lord Atherbourne, but it had been a near thing.

Since that day, he'd resolved to give her time. Let her miss him. Let her want. And then he'd made a plan.

He did not like having to maneuver her into a corner. It was more his mother's nature than his to manipulate others. But she'd left him with little choice.

Right now, there in her eyes, he saw torment. It appeared to pain her, rejecting him. This was not mere lust. She cared for him—he knew she did. He simply did not understand why she refused to admit it.

"Perhaps you do not love me," he rasped, his thumbs stroking her jaw. "Perhaps you dismiss what is between us because you hate my mother or despise the thought of hearing me go on about Ascot and Derby. But you cannot deny this, love." Deliberately, he pressed his hips into hers.

She moaned and cupped the backs of his hands where they held her face.

Ah, yes. She wanted what he could give her. And he would use her weakness to his advantage. He would be as ruthless as necessary. He would do whatever it took.

"I shall make you an offer," he said, lowering his lips to brush lightly over hers. "If you will not consent to be my wife, then let us resolve the unanswered questions between us."

Her breathing had quickened, her breasts cushioning his chest as he explored her face and mouth with tiny, whispering strokes. "Questions?"

"Mmm. How well I can satisfy our mutual cravings, for example."

Again, she moaned, the black centers of her eyes swallowing up sherry brown. "What is your offer?"

"You spend every night during the remainder of the hunt in my bed."

She went rigid against him, her lips parting on an O.

"In exchange," he continued, giving her earlobe a tiny nip. "I shall refrain from informing Sir Mortimer of your shocking fondness for dallying with servants."

She struck his forearm with surprising force. "That is a scurrilous lie, and you know it, you blasted—"

Her violence made him laugh. "I know it *now*. There was a time when I pictured you just like this, lifting your skirt for some faceless stable hand. I came to my senses eventually, of course. But will *he*?"

Again, she shoved at him, forcing him to back away. Grant her room. Let her breathe and think. She was panting now, her cheeks flushed, her eyes flashing. He allowed the space between them, knowing it was only a matter of time.

She paced back and forth across the straw-strewn floor. Every so often, she would stop, shoot him a furious glare, and resume pacing. Distantly, he heard the nicker of one horse and the snort of another. He listened for the crunch of approaching footsteps, glad to hear only the creak of wood protesting the cold.

Finally, she halted, bracing one hand on her hip, the other on the wall. "This is blackmail."

"No. Blackmail implies you don't desire what I am demanding."

"Yes, but the whole point is to persuade me to change my mind about marrying you. Which I will not."

He shrugged as though it did not matter. It did, of course. She was right about his intention.

"You are asking me to be your mistress, Charlie. Even if I agree—"

His heart stalled and surged. Her words were sweet music to his ears.

"—I shall want assurances, as any mistress would."

He schooled his expression. "Such as?"

"You will make no further mention of marriage." Her chin tilted in a challenge. "Either to offer it or to spoil my plans to wed elsewhere."

He didn't like the demand, but her terms were not unreasonable. Besides, his methods of persuasion did not require words. "Done."

"Additionally, no one else must know. I trust you can make appropriate arrangements."

Slowly, he felt a smile curling his lips. She was going to agree. This was easier than he'd dared hope. "There is a cottage in the south wood of Steadwick Park. We'll meet there each evening after your maid has gone to bed."

Several breaths fell between them. Her eyes clung to his while blood pounded everywhere. She would be his. At long bloody last, she would be fully his.

She rushed him so swiftly, he wasn't prepared for it. Slender, feminine hands clutched his lapels and yanked his mouth down to hers, even as her momentum sent him stumbling back against the stall's wooden wall. Sent his skull ricocheting off a post.

"Owf," he mumbled against plump, desperate lips.

"Dreadfully sorry," she gasped before reaching up and stroking the quickly forming lump. "I forgot to mention my final stipulation."

He frowned down at her beautiful, flushed face. "Which is?"

"We begin immediately."

Groaning, he wrapped his hand around her nape and returned her mouth to his. Slid his tongue inside glorious heat. Ground their mouths together like a man starving.

Which he was.

He backed her up, moving them both toward the rear wall, where he could push and grind and delve to his heart's content. Meanwhile, his fingers worked against the pins in her hair, loosening the strands, plunging and clutching cool silk.

Good God, this was the most brilliant bloody idea he'd ever had.

His cock agreed wholeheartedly. It did not care about frigid air or the pain in his head or the fact that they were inside a stable where any groom or servant might chance upon them.

The thoughtless, throbbing thing cared only for her breasts, soft and plump against him.

And her tongue, tangling and wet.

And her hair, spilling in wondrous disarray.

Of course, it would prefer to find its proper place deep and hard inside the heart of her, but that could wait. He could be patient. Bloody hell, he'd already waited more than two years, hadn't he?

Somehow, his cock found the argument unconvincing.

"Charlie," she moaned, her sweet hips working against his. "I've wanted you for too long. I fear I cannot wait another moment."

Good God, this was the worst bloody idea he'd ever had.

His buttocks tightened against the urge to simply lift her skirts, lower his fall, and pound away until nothing existed except the feel of her surrounding him, surrendering to him.

He needed to discipline himself. If he gave her too much, too readily, she'd have no reason to reconsider her previous resistance to his true aims. He did not simply want a good, resounding fuck inside his neighbor's stable, or even twelve nights of ecstasy with a beautiful, passionate mistress.

He wanted Julia to give him forever.

Which would require a great deal of discipline.

An application of sensual skill.

And an unrelenting siege upon her resistance.

"Tonight," he murmured. "I shall meet you here an hour after supper and take you to the cottage."

She nibbled along the edge of his jaw. "Can we not ... right now?"

Yes, his lust shouted. *We can. Right bloody now.*

Ignoring his body's demands, he slid his fingers along her cheek, smiling down at her swollen lips and slumberous eyes and tangled hair. Somehow, he always managed to untidy this supremely tidy woman, whether through kisses or calamity.

"No, love," he said, gentling her with strokes of his thumbs. "We must wait. We require privacy. Hours and hours of it."

Her forehead plunked despairingly against his cravat. "More waiting? Oh, God."

His palm skimmed her back, and he cradled her lightly, careful not to move against her too much. The last thing they needed was additional friction.

Then, he gave a dry chuckle. "My sentiments precisely."

Chapter Eight

"Hmmph. Do not be fooled, Humphrey. The primrose path may be tempting, but its charms tend to wane when you are plucking thorns from your backside."

—THE DOWAGER MARCHIONESS OF WALLINGHAM to her boon companion, Humphrey, upon witnessing his eagerness to leap into unexplored territory.

∞

"WE ARE NEARLY THERE," SAID CHARLIE, HIS TALL FORM A silvery shadow riding a white horse beneath the half-moon's light.

She nodded, although he could not see her, and squeezed her reins. As promised, he'd met her in Dunston's stable, waiting with a white gelding and a smaller brown mare. They had spoken little, the light, rustling wind passing drifts of glittering frost between them as crossed from Fairfield to Steadwick lands, then wound together through dark, looming trees. Even now, there seemed nothing to say, all language crowded out by thrumming anticipation.

Supper had been agonizingly slow, of course. Lady Wallingham's pointed criticisms of Steadwick Hall's footmen—who were "scarcely tall enough, never mind clever enough, to light a taper in a dark room"—and lengthy complaints about the "rubbish roads" and "simpleton innkeepers" between Northumberland and Suffolk required hours of lofty discourse. Additionally, Dunston's cook had decided to increase the number of courses by four. Ostentatious and unnecessary, in Julia's estimation. And *then* three gentlemen had felt the need to regale the other dozen guests with tales of their fowling prowess.

At great, grinding length.

For Julia, every minute had dragged into eternity. Because every minute meant more *waiting*.

Waiting, waiting, waiting.

She was heartily, thoroughly, maddeningly sick of waiting.

For months, it had felt as though her life hung in suspension, putting her in mind of the stuffed American hummingbirds displayed at the British Museum—remarkably lifelike replicas of real animals, positioned as though they still hovered and sipped nectar in a perfumed garden of blooms.

She, too, had been frozen mid-flight, a lifelike replica of a woman, for far too long.

Now, however, Charlie had granted her a reprieve, if only for a few nights. And she would seize this window of time, however brief, in both hands. She would clutch and claw and savor and soak it into her pores.

Perhaps she could never be his wife. But, as she had decided that afternoon, standing inside a dim stable, staring at the man she loved, she could have a taste. For this night, she would come alive long enough to store up a few precious memories. She suspected she would need them in the years to come.

Now, as her mare's hooves crunched along a meandering path beneath leafless oak and weighted pine, she struggled to steady her nerves by counting steps. She was on number five-hundred-and-thirty-two when the cottage came into sight. She didn't know what she'd expected—stone, perhaps. Something similar to her dower cottage. But this cottage was white and brown, half-timbered and thatch-roofed. The windows glowed merrily in their heavy frames, lit gold from the fire within. Set, as it was, within a grove of evergreens dusted by sparkling frost and limned in moonlight, the small house appeared almost magical.

She sighed.

"Do you like it?"

"Oh, yes."

She could almost hear him smiling. "Good."

After helping her dismount, Charlie ushered her inside while he took care of the horses. His absence gave her time to examine the clean, cozy place he had prepared for them. Dominating one wall was a stone-and-timber fireplace far too large for the room. A fire blazed, crackling merrily and turning the interior into a veritable oven.

After the deep chill of their woodland ride, it brought a prickling flush to her skin.

Or perhaps that was the bed, a plain but massive presence along the opposite wall. Canopied in leaf-patterned emerald brocade, it looked like nothing so much as a dark, gigantic oak, felled and squared and assembled into a bower expressly for this golden nest.

Between the bed and the fireplace, a matched pair of winged chairs flanked a round table set with a tea tray.

Tea, she thought. *He even thought of tea. How like my Charlie.*

She wanted to laugh, but the tension in her belly wouldn't permit such a release. With trembling fingers, she lowered her cloak's hood and moved away from the door, her boots carrying her toward the bed with quiet taps against the plank floor.

She swallowed, staring down at the coverlet. Green and gold and shimmering, it was a match for the canopy, but lighter, softer.

Could she be this woman? Her fingers stroked over swirls of embroidery, picturing them sliding instead over his skin. Could she please a man like Charlie?

By the time she and Arthur had been married three years, her husband's attentions had grown all but perfunctory—a kiss or two here, a stroke or two there, a bit of labored breathing, a moment of connection, and then ... sleep. It was not that she hadn't loved him, or that he hadn't loved her. To her knowledge, he'd never taken a mistress, and he'd never shown her anything other than gentleness. They'd been a comfort to each other, warm and easy. Upon occasion, she'd even found a lovely, culminating pleasure while lying with him.

But she'd never burned like this. Not for Arthur. Not for anyone.

Only Charlie.

Her breath caught at the sudden, clenching ache racing from her chest to her belly. She removed her gloves with sharp tugs, then shrugged out of her cloak, gathered and folded the bundle neatly, smoothing the wool over and over.

"Julia."

Her eyes squeezed shut for a moment.

He moved in close behind her—soap and water and crisp winter air, heat and strength and a will that might be hidden, but would not be broken. Lean, solid arms came around her waist. Long-fingered, elegant hands lifted the folded cloak from her grasp. A cool, bristled cheek came to rest against hers.

"Say something, love."

She let a smile take her lips. "The first time you kissed me. Do you remember?"

Her cloak flew, tossed away by an impatient hand to land

God-knew-where. "You were covered in béchamel sauce," he said. "That footman was dismissed, by the by. Although, I must tell you, I never again tasted béchamel without feeling a certain heightened level of interest."

This time, her laugh escaped, low and husky. She remembered every second—her sputtering outrage, his poorly suppressed humor, the argument. And, above all, the moment he'd cornered her in the small chamber where she'd retreated. The moment he'd taken her sauce-spattered face between his beautiful hands and kissed the very breath out of her.

"I wanted more," she said now. "I was furious with you for laughing at my predicament. You know how it upsets me to be ... a mess. But you kissed me. And then I cared for nothing but my greed. I wanted your hands on me. Everywhere. I could not get close enough."

Those hands squeezed her waist almost too tightly, jerking her backside squarely into his prodding hardness before loosening, as though he struggled to control himself.

"This is like nothing I've ever felt," she confessed in a whisper. "A *consuming* kind of hunger. Difficult and peculiar. I want to devour you. Absorb you."

His breath, which had been unnaturally even, stopped. Started again in a long, inward hiss. Panted at her ear. "Julia."

She slid her hands over his, interlacing their fingers across her belly. Swallowing, she continued, glad she did not have to face him while she explained. "I was married to Arthur for nine years."

His chest jerked. His hands dug and curled around hers.

She squeezed back. "I don't know what you're expecting. I am not very ... skilled."

"Bloody hell."

"But I promise you, no woman has ever wanted you more, for that is impossible."

Warm, firm lips sighed against her neck then vibrated with his groan. The sensation of damp heat and the deep, resonant sound of his need sent ripples of pleasure arcing over her body, thrilling her scalp and spine and breasts. Nipples that were already peaked hardened further, aching and burning for him, as they often did. She'd never been capable of hiding her response. It was too flagrant. Too all-consuming.

"I do not need your skill." She'd never heard his voice this deep, this dark. It rumbled in her ear. "Just let me have all of you."

She nodded frantically, unsure what he meant, but ready to give him anything. Everything.

"Stand still, love."

She felt his fingers slide to her back and begin working at her buttons. The tickling sensation along her skin quickened her breath.

"The first time may be ... fast. I hope you won't mind." He was eminently polite, loosening her gown and then the laces of her stays with astounding efficiency. The man was competent at everything he did, and apparently undressing a woman was no exception.

"Fast is ..." She swallowed. Cleared her throat. Wondered what to do with her hands. "Fast is fine. I shan't be keeping time."

He hummed low in his throat. "Rhyming already. Splendid."

"Not on purpose."

"That is what makes it so charming."

"You are laughing at me."

"Not in the slightest, love. I should very much like to remove your bodice now."

Her belly tightened, the needy place between her thighs clenching around an empty ache. "If it pleases you. Shall I take down my hair ... also?" She'd nearly rhymed again. Blast. It was only because her mind scrambled to make sense of her senses. The soap-and-winter smell of him. The fire-and-wine heat of him. The sound and feel and—oh, God—she needed a taste of him. But he kept her facing the bed, staring down at the green and gold swirls of the coverlet.

"Not yet," he rasped. He slid long fingers inside the gaping split of her gown, gently eased the layers of silk velvet and plain cotton and sheer muslin away from her shoulders, down her arms, and across her breasts. The bundled fabric scraped her erect nipples before dropping to hang upon her hips.

She tried to turn, wanting to undress him, to kiss him, but strong hands gripped her waist.

"No," he said again. "Let me ... let me have you, Julia. This once, let me see you and have you as I have dreamed for two bloody years."

She did not know quite what he meant, but his demand was raw, a bit uncontrolled.

"There is this little mole below your ear." Lightly, he stroked one fingertip upon the spot, causing tingling shivers to bloom. "That day, when you served me tea in your drawing room, I envisioned placing my mouth here while I took you." His hand did not remain still. It journeyed down her neck, across her shoulder, and over the ridges of her spine. "And I pondered at great length whether your nipples would match the color of your lips." His substantial chin came to rest upon her shoulder, his cheek caressing hers. Together, they looked down. "I see they do. You simply cannot know how happy this makes me."

Oh, but she could feel it. His hardness was a thick, pulsing, living force where it pressed against her lower back. Then his hands were sliding over her breasts, cupping and squeezing and gathering her back into him. His mouth turned to meet hers. His tongue thrust to challenge and claim hers. His flavor was spice and salt and Charlie.

He stroked and squeezed her fiery, aching nipples between lean, elegant fingers, yanking a sharp moan from her throat. She covered his hands with her own, thrust her hips harder into his, restless and needing him to hurry.

Instead, he pulled his mouth away, breathing in harsh gasps. "Now, love. Now you can take your hair down."

She did so, too frantic to mind the pain in her scalp as she carelessly yanked the pins free, scattering them with a patter on the floor, and jerked clawed hands through the strands.

All the while, as she tended this task, Charlie released one breast and used his free hand to unbutton his fall. Then, he used that same hand to gather the folds of her skirts and drag them up. To caress the flesh of her outer thigh. Then the flesh between her thighs, sensitive fingertips begging entry to explore wet, ready folds and swollen, sensitive nerves. One of those fingertips traced a path between, then around, then, finally, down and down to slide inside the tiniest bit.

She groaned his name.

"Bend forward, love. Onto the bed."

She did not ask why, for she did not care. Everything was liquid heat, clenching and aching and greedy around his invading finger. Firing and sizzling and needy beneath his pinching strokes of her nipple. No, she did not ask why. She simply caught herself on her elbows as she let his strength lower her onto the bed.

Nothing had ever matched this maelstrom of pleasure. Her skin was too tight for her body. Her heart was too powerful for her chest. Her eyes were sightless, utterly lost in halos of amber, gold, and green.

She felt her skirt lift, her buttocks kissed by cooler air. His hand left her center, only to return a moment later. No. Not his hand. This was bigger. Hot and blunt. It notched at her opening, stroked twice along her folds, slow and loving like a kiss. Then, it was pushing. Parting. Thrusting.

The invasion, for all that they had waited two years, happened fully in the space between one breath and the next. One moment she was empty, the next she was filled. Stretched to the edge of pain.

His chest came over her back, the linen of his shirt soft against her naked skin. Gentle lips settled into the spot just beneath her ear. "Are you well, my Julia? I am not hurting you, am I?"

"N-not hurting. Exactly," she gasped the words, struggling to accustom herself to his thickness. The burning stretch at her entrance, the hard pressure deep inside. She was not a virgin, certainly, but it had been years. And Arthur had never been like this.

She worked her hips against the man she loved, squeezed her internal muscles around him. He nuzzled her neck. Licked and suckled. Ran his thumb over the pebbled tip of her nipple. All while remaining still and hard and massively deep inside her.

"Tell me how it feels, love."

She grunted. "Big."

He chuckled, giving her neck another lick. "Too big?"

"No, I ... I think ..."

"Yes?"

"It is just a bit ... overwhelming."

"Hmm. Perhaps if you spread your legs wider."

She made the adjustment.

"Better?"

"Mmm."

"You don't sound certain."

"It is ... ooooh." Her eyes fluttered and drifted shut as he squeezed her nipple with breathtaking firmness. "It is r-rather good, I think."

"Then, I may proceed?"

"Yes."

His lips settled against the curve of her ear. "Good."

The single word was all the warning he gave her before withdrawing to the tip and thrusting fully back inside in a fierce, hard stroke. Then, he repeated the motions, pounding inside with long, driving thrusts. His hand left her breast to grip her hip. The other hand plunged into her hair, gathering and fisting the mass, holding it out of his way while he suckled at the spot just beneath her ear.

The heat of his invasion—the shock and friction—formed a separate reality. All she knew was his body inside hers, the collision of his hips, the stretching fullness. The deep, hard, determined strokes. In this reality, her ache did not abate. It tightened. Fired in her breast and in her core. Wound and coiled and expanded and swelled until she heard herself gasping. Crying his name. Screaming as the pressure of the pleasure became too much. She needed it to go somewhere, and yet it felt trapped inside her.

He was stoking her. Hammering like a blacksmith shaping her into a new form. She tried to tell him it was too much, that she was going to snap like an overstretched line, or split open like an overfilled pillow, but her words came out as "Please. Oh, God, Charlie. Please."

In the end, she did not snap or split. Rather, she filled and stretched until the pleasure was ready to take her, the same way Charlie was taking her—with overwhelming force. The explosion came so suddenly she gave an open-mouthed, silent scream. First, every muscle seized around him, the burst of initial pleasure so steep and sharp, she lost her breath. Then came the suspension, a hovering pause. Then, a bigger explosion, harder and hotter and more powerful than anything she'd ever imagined. It took her like an ocean of fire, a pounding riptide that rolled her in its grip, weakened and strengthened her until she was both dying and being born in the same moment.

As the waves began to ease, she struggled to catch her breath, panting against the soft cushion of gold and green, savoring the feel of Charlie's strength around her, his hands gripping and stroking, his hardness still thrusting, his chest cradling and covering her. She reached back with one hand to caress his nape, loving the texture of his hair, soft and thick between her fingers. She savored him, soaked him in, committed him to memory. The clean spice of his soap. The scrape of his jaw. The sawing of his breath in her ear. The beauty of his hand braced on the bed beside hers.

She felt his crisis approaching. Sensed it in the urgency of his rhythm. Encouraged it with loving contractions of her sheath.

"God, Julia." He gasped the words. Growled something erotic and obscene, a single term she'd heard only once before.

Then, he plunged deep one final time. Held her tight with a steel arm and the curve of a lean body. Groaned and stiffened and breathed her name.

And burst inside her. She was filled with him, taking his pleasure and his seed. Her Charlie was part of her, giving her everything she wanted, including the greatest pleasure she'd ever known.

Everything, that was, except the one thing she could not have—a lifetime of nights just like this.

Chapter Nine

*"Really, Charles. Gloating is unseemly.
Do you imagine you are the first man to achieve
such acquiescence to your every whim?"*

—The Dowager Marchioness of Wallingham to her son, Charles, upon discovering his unusual talent for winning favor with her boon companion, Humphrey.

∞

By the time Charles had delivered her to Fairfield, Julia once again had been a mess—lips plump, hair untidy and hastily pinned, cheeks reddened from contact with his face. He'd helped her fasten her gown, of course, but the thing had been wrinkled and rumpled until it was obvious how she had spent her night.

It was splendid. He was having trouble stifling his grin.

She, along with seven of Dunston's guests, had come to Steadwick Hall for a visit. Looking at her now, her long, white neck craned to view his vast, two-story library, he fancied no one would suspect this neat, composed woman of being such an erotic creature. Her gown was soft, crimson wool, perfectly pressed. Her hair was tightly secured, her hands clasped modestly at her waist. But, he noted, she must have felt his gaze upon her, for a lovely pink had flooded her cheeks.

"Have you considered one of the Aldridge girls? Neither possesses a jot of cleverness, but their mother birthed two sets of twins. *Two*. Fecundity compensates for a great many failings."

He rolled his eyes at his mother. The moment the company from Fairfield had arrived, she'd made a show of playing hostess, ordering his servants about, describing the purpose of each room to "her" guests.

"Mother, I have no wish to marry a girl who was exiting the cradle at the same time I was exiting Oxford. Fecundity notwithstanding."

He sensed her irritation. "Well, if you must fixate upon a widow of more advanced years, perhaps Lady Turnwicke will tempt your appetites."

Chuckling, he shot her a glance. "Speaking of fecund, eh?"

Her narrowed gaze implied she found him more vexing than humorous. She looked as though she wished to stamp her foot. "I see no reason she may not birth an eighth child. The first seven came readily enough."

He hummed a neutral response, clasped his hands behind his back, and resumed watching Julia. She was laughing with an incredulous Olive Willoughby at something inside a book. How long would it take her to rearrange his library after he made her the mistress of Steadwick Hall? Two days. Perhaps three. Longer if he managed to keep her occupied with other, more pleasurable pursuits.

"Stop that at once," his mother snapped. "I cannot bear your incessant, unreasoning good humor another moment."

He raised a brow. "Ah, yes. Happiness. Most unseemly. I do beg your pardon, my lady."

She dismissed his sarcasm with lift of her chin. "As you should. I recognize that expression. Your father wore it often."

Covering his sudden laugh with a cough, he tightened his lips on another grin.

"Dally all you wish, Charles. Install her as your mistress, if you so choose. But you would do well to recall marriage's primary purpose and all the ways she is poorly suited for such a role."

He had no doubt of whom she spoke. From the beginning, his mother had wavered between elation that Julia had caused him to reconsider remarriage and dismay at the various calamities of their courtship. Most recently, she had launched a campaign of dissuasion, encouraging him to find a younger, less "disastrous" woman to marry.

As always, her criticisms of Julia chafed his temper like nothing else. "Have a care how you speak about her, Mother. Soon, she will be your daughter-in-law."

Peculiar alarm flared over her features. "Has she consented?"

"Not yet. But she will."

Last night had been just the beginning. A glorious, magnificent, explosive beginning. She had given herself beautifully, over and over. Tonight, he would turn pleasure into persuasion, force her to acknowledge her proper place in his life. By the end, if he was careful, he had little doubt she would reach the correct conclusion—she belonged with him.

However, that particular strategy could wait for nightfall. This morning, he intended to tempt her in a different way. With Steadwick Park.

"Pardon me, Mother," he said, starting toward the beautiful woman gowned in fetching red wool. "A certain widow requires my attention."

HE WAS MANIPULATING HER. DELIBERATELY. METHODICALLY. Julia knew it, and yet could not fault his strategy.

It was working.

"Naturally, my energies have been directed toward expanding the stables," he said casually. The dratted, clever man stood beside her, hands clasped at his back. He shot a considering glance at the upper tier of rich, dark bookshelves and clicked his tongue. "No time at all for putting the library in proper order, never mind the kitchens. I'll wager there are rooms in this place that haven't been dusted in two years. A shame, really."

Her hands clenched briefly. She longed to tell him to go to the devil. Or to corner his housekeeper and begin coordinating a sane cleaning regimen. This place—a splendidly symmetrical Palladian masterpiece—was nearly as tempting as its owner.

"Your stables are, indeed, magnificent, my lord." Although her words were intended as a distraction, they were no less true. Upon viewing the stables earlier, she had marveled at both their size and cleanliness. Each block, of which there were six, housed twenty stalls. Inside each stall was another example of Charlie's unparalleled talent for recognizing, acquiring, and breeding prime horseflesh.

"Hmm. We were forced to eliminate the walled garden to make room for the third building. Now, I am at a loss as to where to relocate it." He shrugged and sighed. "Perhaps the north side of the house will do."

She swallowed, holding her breath to stop herself from responding. The words begged to be uttered, but she refused to give him the satisfaction.

"You cannot put a walled garden in the shade," some other, less controlled Julia said. "Nothing will grow. Place it south of the fish pond, near the orangery. You will have to remove several trees, but the garden will receive full sun throughout the day, and it is a short walk from the kitchens."

His widening grin spoke of triumph. "Eminently sensible."

She gritted her teeth. Blast. Not only had he spent the entire night ravishing her into a blissful puddle, he had apparently decided to exploit *all* her weaknesses in a similarly ruthless fashion.

"You should wear that gown this evening," he said with idle nonchalance. "The color is most ... becoming against your skin."

Her heart stuttered in her chest. "I shall wear what I like."

Again, he grinned as though he'd won. "Fair enough." He strolled away, all but whistling.

Inside, she seethed. He knew precisely what he was doing, and it wasn't *fair* at all. How was she to resist him? At this rate, she would be begging him to marry her before the week was out.

Besides which, who contemplated placing a walled garden on the north end of a house? Pure foolishness.

Thankfully, over the next hour, he kept his distance, showing her and the others around Steadwick Hall with his usual calm, quiet assurance. After the library came twin drawing rooms flanking an elaborate rotunda, then the massive dining room with its blue silk walls, then the long gallery at the rear of the house, where portraits of his antecedents mingled with grand landscapes and the occasional glossy-coated thoroughbred.

It was there, at the west end of the gallery, where Lady Wallingham approached her. Olive and Helen had wandered away to view a new Turner while Julia admired a portrait of an unsmiling Lady Wallingham holding a white-gowned, dark-haired infant upon her lap. Charlie, of course.

"He had the Bainbridge chin even then," came the sonorous voice from beside her elbow. "I had hoped he might avoid the affliction."

Julia smiled gently and returned her gaze to the painting.

The babe's arms were outstretched toward his mother, and while the woman's eyes might be glaring imperiously at the artist, her hands cradled the boy's back protectively. "I quite like it, actually," she replied. "Other chins seem weak and insubstantial by comparison."

The dowager sniffed. "That is only because you are besotted."

Julia blinked.

"Oh, do not pretend with me, girl. I am neither senile nor blind."

She swallowed before replying, "I have never denied my admiration for your son."

"Admiration." The old woman spat the word. "You are in love with him. He knows it. I know it. Even your befuddled botanist knows it."

"Sir Mortimer? How—"

"A woman who spends an entire supper staring longingly in another man's direction diminishes her matrimonial allure a fair bit, wouldn't you agree?"

Pressing her lips together, Julia glanced down the length of the gallery to where Sir Mortimer explained to Helen why the flora depicted in one of the landscapes was all wrong. Helen shook her head and chuckled, teasing him about being a stickler for accuracy while entirely missing the point of artistic endeavor. Sir Mortimer smiled down at her, his eyes glowing with affection.

"Find another prospect, Lady Willoughby," said the dowager. "It appears Sir Mortimer has already done so."

Her heart squeezing until the pain lodged in her throat, Julia wondered how she could have missed the signs. Helen. Dear, dear Helen was eminently better suited to Sir Mortimer than she. And, yet, in her haste to secure her own future, she had forced Helen to set aside what Julia now realized was a late-blooming romance.

Lady Wallingham was right, yet again. Julia must find another prospect.

Charlie. Only ever Charlie.

She resisted the mutinous voice, clamped tight and held her breath until it stopped its pleading chant.

"And you may forget about Charles. Upon your departure, I've little doubt he will find comfort elsewhere. Then, perhaps, he may fulfill his proper duty to produce an heir, and your association will come to an ignominious, yet welcome, end."

Seemingly satisfied with her final, acidic declaration, Lady Wallingham turned away, her blue velvet gown swishing, her white, feathery plume bobbing above her white, turbaned head. It was the same sort of arrogant, high-flown statement she'd made the previous spring, while Julia's hands had shaken hard enough to spill scalding tea on her lap.

While her heart had broken hard enough to split her in half.

The dragon had been brutal then, and she was brutal now.

Just lately, however, Julia had had her fill of dragons.

"My lady," she called, watching the dowager turn with arched brows and studied nonchalance. Julia approached her slowly, halting a foot away and meeting a haughty green gaze with unvarnished truth. "I love your son."

A sniff. "Obviously."

"No. You don't understand. I am not merely *in love* with him. This is not some girlish fancy that will disappear with time. Frankly, that might be preferable."

Green eyes blinked and narrowed. A delicate chin tilted.

"I love him more than my own happiness. More than my own life. I *know* I can never bear him children. I know that, my lady. I have no need of reminders." Oh, how these words hurt. She could scarcely think them without wanting to weep, and saying them aloud, especially to this woman, was killing her. But she must.

Although the dragon became a silent, swirling blur, Julia did not look away from her. Instead, she smiled, swallowing her sadness, speaking through it. "He deserves to be a father. I have never known a more patient man. A better man. He will love and protect his children with all his strength. He's learned that much from you." She wiped impatiently at her damp cheeks and let her voice harden. "But please. Please do not speak to me as though this is anything less than my death. Despite everything, I go to the gallows gladly. For *his* happiness. Not mine. And certainly not yours."

With that, Julia left the Dowager Marchioness of Wallingham standing motionless in a shaft of light and, for once in her long life, at a loss for words.

Chapter Ten

"You say 'dragon' as though I should take offense. If I am not mistaken, dragons are supremely adept at securing that which belongs to them. Perhaps those who seek to offer insult should instead inquire after their own deficiencies in that quarter."

—The Dowager Marchioness of Wallingham to Lady Gattingford during a luncheon filled with gossip, slander, and a rather lovely pot of tea.

∞

That night, the wind strengthened to a gale, sifting trees and stirring billows of glittering frost outside the cottage's mullioned windows. Julia fancied they might see snow before the end of the hunt.

Strong arms locked around her naked back. Gentle lips preceded a playful tongue across her breast. "Would you care for more tea, my dear?"

She laughed. She could not help it. The man was insatiable.

When they'd arrived earlier, she had needed him badly. Needed to hold his face between her hands and feel his mouth upon hers. Needed to take him inside her and find her pleasure. Needed to lay her cheek upon his chest and listen to his heart. She had done all that, and he had simply held her for the longest time, saying nothing. They had lain together in the bower bed, listening to the wind outside, basking in the rhythm of their heartbeats and the comfort of shared heat.

He hadn't asked her what was wrong, but she knew he sensed it. Charlie always perceived her distress, even when she was careful. Tonight, she hadn't been careful. She'd been desperate.

Her conversation with Lady Wallingham had torn her open again. She'd needed Charlie to stitch her back together.

Later, after she'd dozed for a while, Charlie had risen from the bed and moved to the table, his lean, long body a mélange of defined muscles and dark, swirling hair. Golden firelight caught in the silver at his temples, shone on the thick, semi-hard staff between his thighs. She'd shifted restlessly against the sheets, her body beginning to melt for him again.

Grinning devilishly over his shoulder, he'd beckoned her to join him. "Come, love. Pour us some tea, won't you?"

She'd protested that she was naked.

"Precisely," he'd purred.

She'd served him tea as though they were in a Mayfair drawing room. Naked. Within minutes, he'd lost all patience for the game, and had promptly transferred her to his lap.

Now, she straddled his thighs upon the winged leather chair, his hardness buried to the hilt, his mouth feasting upon her neck and her nipples. His hands coursed down her back to squeeze her hips then her buttocks.

"Oh, Charlie," she groaned, clutching his neck and loving the feel of him, hard and full inside her. She laid kisses along his brow, down those aristocratic cheekbones, and across his substantial chin. She wanted to memorize him. Every square inch. She wanted to take him with her when she left, merged with her skin and blood and bones.

He pulled back until his eyes caught hers. The green was fired emerald beneath low, glowering brows. His chest worked against his breaths, against her breasts. He reached up with a single thumb and touched her cheek. It came away wet.

"Bloody hell, Julia," he whispered. "Tell me."

It gathered suddenly. Everything she'd been guarding. It pressed and pushed and swelled inside her chest. Abruptly, the barrier broke, and a gulping sob escaped. She covered her mouth with both hands to stop it. But it wouldn't be stopped.

She gasped and lost her grip.

He cradled her face between his beautiful hands. Lowered her head to lay tender lips on her temple. "Tell me," he repeated. "The time has come, love."

It took long minutes for her to speak. When she finally had sufficient control of her breathing, she shuddered and clung to his neck, resting her damp face in the crook of his shoulder. "I watched him ..." She breathed against Charlie's skin. "Long before he died, I watched him leave me."

Charlie remained still and silent, stroking her back with patient hands. Listening. He'd always listened so well. It was one of the things she loved most.

"Month by month. Year by year. I could not ... give him what he had every right to expect. We would hope. Then, we would be disappointed. Over and over. He never blamed me. But I watched a part of him—the part that w-wanted me—wither."

More stroking, rhythmic and smooth. More silence.

Charlie's patience steadied her. Gave her courage.

"I am barren, Charlie. And I cannot watch while that fire disappears from your eyes. I will not survive watching you look upon another man's children and regret the choice you made.

This is *my* burden to carry, not yours. That is why I cannot marry you. But I do love you, my darling. Never doubt it. I love you so very much."

It eased her to say the words, as though her pretense had been a slow poison, and she'd been purged at long last. She laid a tiny kiss on his throat and snuggled closer.

The silence stretched. His hands continued their long, steady path. Up and down. Neck to hips. Again and again. While she felt soothed by the motions, his muscles were not particularly relaxed. In fact, his presence inside her remained hard as steel. She was surprised he hadn't withdrawn the moment she'd launched into her ridiculous, tearful confession. A sobbing woman could not be terribly arousing.

Except right now he was aroused. Quite so.

Slowly, she slid her arms from around his neck and down his dark-furred chest. Pressing lightly, she straightened and looked at him.

And what she saw stole her breath.

Charles Bainbridge, the fourteenth Marquess of Wallingham, was resoundingly, utterly, incandescently furious.

***

HER FACE WAS WREATHED IN RED. PERHAPS IT WAS THE firelight or the ravages of weeping. But he suspected it was his vision. Right now, everything was red.

"Charlie?"

He reached up to smooth her hair. That long, lustrous hair with shades of honey and champagne.

She sniffed. "Why are you angry?"

He did not answer. His hand cupped her nape. His thumb stroked her jaw.

Her breasts were wondrous. He examined them with a

careful eye. Peach nipples that turned a delicate, rosy hue when she was aroused. Or when he suckled them, which amounted to the same thing. Lush and full, those breasts were rounded pears tipped with sweet, miniature peaches. He found them delectable.

Her skin pleased him, as well. Rose-scented and velvety, it needed only the barest brush of his bristled jaw to redden. She was exquisitely sensitive. Delicate, even.

Which was why he must control his reactions now.

He could not give in to his rage or take her the way he wanted—hard and pounding and without mercy. He swallowed and breathed against the urge. His cock, of course, centered snugly inside her sheath, did not approve of his caution.

It wanted to claim her.

That was it. He wanted to claim what was his. For, she did not belong to Arthur Willoughby, who had obviously been an imbecile. It was good he was dead. Charles was glad—yes, glad—for two reasons. First, because Julia could now be his. And second, if the man hadn't been dead, he'd want to kill him for hurting her. Neither of these reasons was *reasonable* in the slightest. They were primitive madness.

Still, they were merely the roots of his current rage. The rest of it was fury at her. Julia. For loving him and lying about it. For leaving him without granting him a say. She hadn't bothered to ask whether he wanted children or whether he could accept her barrenness. She had simply decided she must marry another man. To spare *him*.

The absurdity would be laughable if it were not so painful.

He stroked her hair again. "You will never—*never*—marry anyone else, Julia. Is that very clear?"

Bloody hell. His rage was speaking for him.

And once it had begun, it wanted more.

Sherry eyes rounded. "Er—Charlie? I—I thought you ... understood. I must marry someone, for my portion is not sufficient to purchase a cottage of my own, and I simply cannot remain at the dower cottage. I have become moldy cheese, and it is untenable."

He frowned. "Moldy cheese?"

"Sir Mortimer is no longer an option. I believe he and Helen are ... well, let it suffice to say, my plans have changed. And, before you ask, I do not have anyone else in mind as yet. Pleasant widowers with multiple male offspring are not as common as you might think."

"Julia."

"Yes?"

"You will not marry anyone else. No other man—widower or otherwise—will ever be inside you. No other man will ever look upon your breasts or watch you serve him tea whilst naked or take you with the kind of wild fury I feel right now. Because you are mine. And that is the end of this particular topic."

Her eyes softened. Turned dark and rich with a return of tenderness. And lust. He was most glad of that.

"Charlie," she breathed, her fingers stroking his hair. "I can never give you children."

"It does not matter."

"You only think so because you want me right now. But time will pass, and other lords—your friends—will have sons to carry on their titles and make them intolerably boastful. It may not matter the first time or the second. But how long, Charlie? How many years before you look upon what you could have had and begin to regret—"

"Do you want the truth?" His voice was harsh and raw, for he had nothing left to discipline it.

She bit her lip and nodded.

"I never expected to have children. I never expected—or wanted—to marry again."

She stroked him with soft fingers and what felt like sympathy. "Because you loved your first wife. I know."

He shook his head. "Wrong. I despised her, Julia."

Blinking, she frowned and opened her mouth to speak. Closed

it. Opened again. "You—but I—everyone thought that you—"

"Mourned. For fifteen years? Only sentimental fools believe that rubbish." Perhaps he sounded like his mother. He did not care. He'd allowed society to believe what it wanted, but his marriage had been a torturous hell for two years before Susannah died, mercifully, of a fever. "The woman was stark staring mad. I managed as well as I could, kept her largely confined to Grimsgate. But half the time, she was curled up in her bed sobbing about absolute trivialities, and the other half, she was bedding the footman or throwing a bloody fete and behaving as though she'd been crowned Prinny's successor."

The O of Julia's lips made him want to kiss her. She, on the other hand, wanted to pet his hair and soothe him. "My poor Charlie. How trying that must have been."

"Yes, well, it was ages ago."

"But you decided not to marry. Ever."

"I liked my life as it was."

"And, naturally, your mother forced the issue, demanded you marry to carry on your lineage."

He grunted.

"Perhaps her insistence was a factor in your resistance?"

"You are rhyming again. And yes, probably. I do not enjoy dancing upon her strings."

She grinned, her dimples showing. "You manage her quite masterfully, you know. Such strength of will is most ... impressive."

"I have had long practice."

Earlier, he had yearned to kiss her. Now, instead, she kissed him. Sweetly. Holding his jaw steady so she could lick and suckle and tease and tempt. Her sheath caressed him where they were still joined, squeezing and pleasuring his cock.

"Do you know what else is impressive?" she panted against his lips. "The fact that you remain hard and ready for me, even while comforting me in my distress and calmly discussing weighty subjects."

"Julia."

She nibbled his chin. "Hmm?"

"I am going to lift you now and take you quite forcefully upon the table."

"Oh, but what about the tea?"

"It may spill on the floor."

"We will cause a terrible mess."

"Yes."

She sighed and gave him another loving squeeze. "Then I suggest we get started."

He lifted her with one arm, hoisted her backside onto the edge of the table and promptly shoved the tea tray to the floor. It caused a dreadful clatter before the pot settled on its side, splattering brown liquid in a wide arc across the planks. He did not care.

Astoundingly, neither did she. Julia—his tidy, orderly Julia—laid back upon the wooden table with swollen lips and mussed hair and flushed nipples. And she smiled. Glowed. Welcomed him with open arms.

He gripped her thighs and pulled her tighter against his hips. He gave her a small thrust to test her readiness. She sighed and closed her eyes, arching her back in a graceful preen.

God, she was beautiful.

Velvety skin and peach nipples. Sherry eyes that crinkled when she laughed. He had never wanted a woman like this. She thought his stamina impressive, but it was only the product of his extraordinary lust for her.

He bent forward to lick a beaded nipple, savoring her gasp, her grasp of his hair. She was slick around his cock. Wet but not yet fully ready. Drawing her nipple deeper into his mouth, he suckled with firm pulls and gentle nibbles.

Then he made her gasp with a deeper, harder thrust between her thighs.

"Oh!"

He lifted her knees higher, draped her legs over his arms. Thrust again.

"Good God, Charlie."

Better. Yes, she was nearly there.

He withdrew almost entirely and sank fully inside her tight heat, stretching her sheath and staking his claim. Once. And again. And again. She signaled her approval with a series of deep, throaty moans.

"Julia."

"Oh, God."

"You belong to me, love. Say you understand." Now the light was brighter in the room, the fire casting her skin in gold.

"I am yours, Charlie. I will always be yours."

Triumph exploded in his chest. For long minutes, all he could do was take her. Hard and long. Hard and deep. Hard and pounding and unrelenting. She wrapped her legs around his back, giving him the angle he needed to go even deeper, to increase the friction of his slick cock against the pouting nub swollen with her need.

He loved hearing her gasps and moans. He loved pleasuring her with his cock and his mouth. He loved smelling the sweet blend of roses and woman and hot, velvety skin. He loved feeling the warning ripples of her fiery implosion, the wringing of her sheath as it convulsed around him, the clawing of her hands on his scalp and nape and back.

Most of all, he loved taking the woman he loved and releasing a firestorm of pleasure inside her, pouring from her to him, from him to her in surging, gushing waves. He savored watching her eyes glow for him like dark, golden flames. Hearing her throaty, seductive laughter as they heaved panting, desperate breaths together in the aftermath, touching and stroking as though to stop would tear them to pieces.

"We've made a proper mess, my lord." She kissed his cheek and then his mouth as he lifted her from the table, his legs weakened but thankfully steady.

He carried her to the bed and answered, "Yes, love. A proper mess, indeed."

Chapter Eleven

"In the end, I am your mother, Charles.
I shall always be your mother,
however you may wish it were not so."

—The Dowager Marchioness of Wallingham to her son,
Charles, in the third iteration of a letter destined
for the kindling basket.

∞

The snow arrived on the fourteenth morning of Dunston's hunt. Rather than diffident flurries, it came in a cascade of sparkling white, coating fields and branches, stables and cottages in a thick hush.

The whole thing put Charles in a foul mood. Trudging up the drive toward Steadwick Hall, he listened to the distinct, muffled crunch of his boots traversing what must be fourteen inches of the stuff. Fortunately, apart from the weather, he had few complaints. He'd been gratified by his meeting with the vicar that morning, and matters were proceeding well with Julia.

Quite well.

He almost smiled, recalling their long, wondrous nights at the cottage. She was an exceptional woman—passionate and loving, sensual and sweet, charming and wise. And just a bit odd. He liked that.

But he did not like the snow. At this rate, his mother would refuse to leave until the spring thaw. He'd been prepared for her to remain at Steadwick past Christmas, but he and Julia would soon be wed, and he'd hoped his mother would depart shortly thereafter so he and his new bride could be alone.

He cast a glare up at the offending clouds. A fat snowflake landed in his eye. "Blast," he muttered, blinking it away and tugging at his hat's brim. Deciding it was no use cursing the fates, he hunched his shoulders and quickened his pace.

His butler met him inside the entrance hall, taking his damp hat and snowy greatcoat with a daft look of delight. "Extraordinary to have such an abundance of snow this early in December, is it not, my lord? Makes everything seem fresh and new, I daresay."

Rather than spoiling the man's exuberance, Charles simply nodded. "I suppose."

"Where have you been, boy?" His mother's voice echoed off russet walls and white columns.

He turned a frown upon her. "Out."

"In a blizzard? What could be so important?" She wore green velvet today, giving her eyes an unusual intensity. In one hand, she held her lorgnette, in the other, a stack of papers. Letters, most likely, from her many contacts around England. Mother did like to stay informed.

"I had matters to attend," he said, starting toward his study.

Oddly enough, she followed. "I must speak with you."

"Perhaps later, Mother." Arrangements for a wedding this time of year were challenging, particularly if he wished to provide her with roses. He knew of at least one neighbor who grew them year-round in his greenhouse, but Charles wished Julia to have red—deep, dark red roses. She would be pleased at the surprise, he thought. Only last night, she had been describing how she adored the red roses in her garden at the dower cottage.

"No. Not later. Now."

Ignoring his mother's bark, he continued past the south staircase and down the corridor. He must locate a source for red roses. Perhaps Sir Mortimer would have a suggestion. He nearly laughed aloud at the irony.

"She is leaving, Charles."

He halted at the threshold of his study's open door. Inside the oak-paneled room, a fire crackled. It was the only sound he heard, apart from his heartbeat. That was rather thunderous at the moment.

"Leaving?" he said softly, pivoting to face her. "Where would she go? We are to be married."

Her lips pursed and tightened. "Evidently, she has formed alternative plans."

He walked toward his mother, aware he was looming and not giving a fig. "How would you know such a thing?"

"Alicia."

"Your new lady's maid?"

"Woefully incompetent at selecting an appropriate pair of slippers, but quite useful for ferreting information. She befriended Lady Willoughby's maid. Peggy, I believe."

"And?"

"Peggy has been instructed to prepare for their departure in two days, when Lady Willoughby will return with her family to Bedfordshire."

He searched his mother's eyes, wondering how far to trust

her. It was true that her sources seldom proved false—she was a stickler in that regard. But Julia had discarded the notion of marrying Sir Mortimer. Surely she understood Charles's intentions. He had spoken them plainly enough. And, every time he insisted that she belonged to him and no one else, she had smiled and kissed him.

But she had not said yes. She had not promised she would stay.

A wrinkle appeared between his mother's white brows. It spoke of concern. Sorrow. "Can you not turn your affections to someone better, Charles? Why must you batter away at this stone when there are jewels stacked so conveniently within reach?"

"Julia is the only treasure I shall ever desire."

"Don't be such a fool. She is barren. And thirty."

"I don't care that she is barren. She belongs to me and I to her. And what has her age to do with anything? You were thirty-two when I was born."

Her eyes sharpened and snapped. "Precisely. Good heavens, boy, do you not comprehend I am trying to spare you the pain your father and I endured?"

His heart gave a peculiar squeeze. His mother rarely spoke of her struggles during the years before his birth. She'd buried four babes, all stillborn, and suffered at least three miscarriages before bringing him into the world. She had lost hope of ever producing the Wallingham heir when, for an eighth time, she'd found herself with child.

To ensure his survival, she had taken to her bed for the last four months of her pregnancy. Even with those precautions, he'd come several weeks early. It had been a near thing. He'd often thought she'd willed him into existence. His mother was formidable, in part, because she refused tragedy the privilege of reveling in her defeat.

"Would you take it back, Mother?" he asked, knowing the answer before the words left him. "Had you foreseen the struggles you and Father would face together, would you have chosen someone else? Someone you loved less?"

Those eyes, so like his own, fired with shocking anguish. Her proud chin trembled. She retreated a step. Then another.

He hadn't meant to hurt her. He, of all people, knew how profoundly she had loved her husband. One of his most vivid recollections was of them together. As a boy of four or five, he'd been hiding in a corner of Grimsgate's east library, pretending to be a stowaway on one of England's mighty warships. His father had entered—looking a great deal like the man Charles now saw in his shaving mirror every morning—conversing patiently, rationally with Mother about the dangers of meddling. Mother had shouted her frustration with his calm demeanor, demanding to know how he could be sanguine when the "entirety of London is suffering a stupefying malady of the mind." Father had laughed. She had been furious. Then, she had kissed him. Passionately. Clutching his coat in her fists. Pulling at his hair and letting him lift her by the waist. Then, she'd whispered in his ear while Father had carried her out of the room. At the time, Charles hadn't known—or wanted to know—what it was all about. All he'd known was that Mother loved Father with every ounce of force she could bring to bear. And from the beginning, she had loved Charles with the same ferocity.

But that did not excuse her behavior. She'd schemed and meddled and manipulated until his only choice was to either hand her the reins or take his horse and travel a different path. His preference for the latter option had frustrated her for almost two decades. When he was young, he'd married Susannah because Mother had been certain they were "an ideal match." That had been the last time he had let her make a decision that was rightly his.

Now, standing before him with her agony laid bare, she tightened her mouth and mustered her anger, donning it like a new turban. "How dare you ask me such a thing, boy," she snapped. "The difference between my choice of husband and your choice of wife is precisely this: I had no way to foresee our difficulties. You are inviting yours to take up residence in your bedchamber."

"And that is my choice to make. Not yours."

"It would seem she is making it for you."

"Not if I have anything to say about it."

"Obstinate whelp. Well, go on then. Attempt your persuasions *again* if you must. I doubt you will find any greater success this time. She appeared rather set upon martyrdom when last we spoke."

Suspicions prickled along his skull. "Spoke? What have you done, Mother?"

She blinked. Arched a brow. "I don't know what you mean."

"If you have coerced Julia into leaving me—"

"Nothing of the sort. She made her decisions of her own accord." She sniffed. "I merely pointed her in the direction of that which is patently obvious. She is barren. You are in need of an heir."

"I have an heir," he growled. "He is your nephew. Perhaps you remember him."

She gave a snort. "I would rather not."

"Bloody hell." He drew a breath and ran a hand through his hair, paced into the middle of the study and stood for a full minute.

How can she think of leaving me? he wondered, his gut churning.

He didn't realize he'd spoken the question aloud until his mother answered, "Perhaps she loves you enough to want your happiness more than her own."

He turned, his breathing fast, his mind scrambling for purchase. "She *is* my happiness," he said baldly, uncaring that it sounded like a plea. "I cannot lose her, Mother."

For the longest time, she simply gazed back at him, her proud chin elevated, her eyes wandering his face with slow deliberation. Then, he watched her stroll calmly to the polished oak desk, place her lorgnette and letters upon its surface, and pause before returning to him. She was a small woman. Tiny, really. And growing more delicate with each passing year. When she was this close, she had to crane her neck to meet his eyes.

"Then you shall not, my son," she said softly. "Now, let us see to it, hmm?"

―⁂―

"Do you suppose we will have to delay our departure?" Olive queried, peering out the window of Fairfield's lovely green parlor. Her fingers brushed at the silk draperies. "It is a dreadful lot of snow."

"Unlikely," Helen replied from her perch near the fireplace, mumbling around her embroidery needle. She took it between her fingers once again so she could finish speaking. "Snow rarely lasts more than a few days before the rain returns."

I wish it would last forever, thought Julia, raising her tea to her lips and finding it both too hot and too weak. *Then perhaps I could stay here. Spend every night in our cottage bower, lying in his arms.* The notion brought a wistful smile to her lips.

"The hunt has been enjoyable, of course," continued Helen. "However, I admit to pining for my own bed. Additionally, Sir Mortimer persuaded Miles to make a brief stop at his residence in Cambridgeshire. He claims to have specimens which bloom in September and wilt come January. I should like to see them, for they cannot be as splendid as he claims."

Julia had been heartened by the growing affection between Helen and Sir Mortimer. Only last evening, Helen had entered Julia's chamber and, with girlish sincerity, had expressed her gratitude for Julia's decision to cease her pursuit of the baronet.

"I did not wish to spoil your plans," Helen had said, squeezing Julia's hands in hers and grinning until her eyes fairly danced. "But I am ever so glad you changed them." Then, blushing like a chit of nineteen, she had whispered, "He kissed me, my dear lady. And it was wondrous. Sir Mortimer Spalding. Who would think it?"

Julia had hugged her tightly and told her dearest friend how pleased she was for Helen's happiness.

If I could only secure such happiness for myself.

Blast. She was turning morose. Self-pity was tiresome, and she'd grown weary of the hard ache at the center of her chest.

To nurse the pain, she took another sip of too-weak tea and leaned her shoulder against the window casing while contemplating the vagaries of loving a man one should not have.

Should not? Why not?

Because he deserves the chance to have children.

The argument had repeated over and over in her head, the echoes growing louder with each passing day.

Each passing night.

Oh, the nights.

She would stroke his dark brow, lay her head on his chest, listen to his heartbeat, and wonder if leaving was really for the best. She would hear him laugh at one of her unintentional rhymes and wonder if any other man would find them so delightful. She would listen to his newest plans for Steadwick's stables, watch him ride a glossy Thoroughbred with deft grace, or lay beside him as he shared his memories of hiding from his governess inside the vastness of Grimsgate Castle. And she would wonder how she could ever live without this man.

She still did not know.

"Do you suppose we should ask Cook for more than one pudding at Christmas, Julia?" Olive asked, coming to stand beside her.

Julia gave her a small smile. "If it pleases you."

Olive frowned, the tight curls around her face bouncing as she shook her head. "Have you no opinion on the matter?"

"It is your home, dear," she said gently, patting Olive's

shoulder. "Your table and your Cook. Therefore, your decision."

It was true. Julia did not belong at Willoughby Manor any more than she belonged with Sir Mortimer.

I belong with Charlie.

She tried to stifle the voice again, but it persisted. *Charlie. Charlie. Charlie. I belong with Charlie.*

"... devil do you think you ... about?" The distinctive trumpet of a dragon echoed beyond the parlor doors. It grew louder as the tapping of boots neared. "Kindly remove your hand, sir, or I assure you, it shall be removed rather more permanently. Where in blazes does Dunston hire his footmen? Newgate? The cheek!"

The doors swung open, and a red-faced, steely-eyed young footman waved Lady Wallingham into the room. "The parlor, my lady."

She waggled her fingers at the young man. "Go away. Find something useful to do. Acquire a new position, perhaps."

Julia blinked once. Twice. She'd never seen the dowager quite this ... bedraggled. The woman's green gown was soaked from hem to mid-skirt. The feather on her riding hat lay limp and sad over the brim's edge, dripping melted snow onto her shoulder.

"Lady Willoughby!"

Olive answered first. "Yes, my lady?"

A dainty, cold-reddened nose lifted higher. "Not you." Green eyes collided with Julia's. "Lady Willoughby."

Still flummoxed by the dowager's appearance, Julia took several seconds to reply, and then she could only produce one word. "Yes?"

"We must speak. The matter is grave."

Her blood froze. Cold tightened everything to stillness. Sound disappeared. Air disappeared. Everything disappeared except what she needed to know. "Ch—Charlie. Is he ... did something happen?"

"You! You have happened. Calamity? Bah! A catastrophe is what you are."

Julia's stomach twisted so hard, she nearly bent double. "Is he hurt? Please." She stumbled forward, stretching a hand toward the dragon. "I must know."

"Of course he is hurt. You have lured him with your questionable wiles into a state of madness. He knows of your imminent departure. He is distraught."

She gulped air into her lungs. Her hand dropped and flattened over her middle. "Distraught. Not ... injured."

"My son is hale and healthy, apart from his unfortunate affliction."

Julia waited.

The dowager sniffed. "That would be you."

Sighing, Julia shook her head. "I don't understand. Is this not what you wanted?"

White brows arched into an imperious frown. "Good heavens. One would think a woman of your age would have developed a spine by now. What does it matter what I want? Charles wants *you*. How dare you threaten to leave my son!"

Julia glanced around the room in bewilderment. Olive and Helen wore twin expressions of rapt fascination. Apart from them, the room was empty. Except for Julia. And the madwoman, of course.

"He is, even now, charging out into this atrocious blizzard, risking his neck in a senseless, drunken attempt to win your affections once more."

"Drunken?"

"Well, perhaps not drunken. Although, he is fond of French cognac, you know."

"Yes, I ..."

"This will not stand. You will repair my son at once, Lady Willoughby. At. Once."

Julia wanted to oblige her. She wanted to run to him. Stay with him. Where she belonged.

Her eyes dropped to where her hand lay flat over her belly. "I cannot provide him with an heir, my lady." Her voice was a hoarse whisper. She lifted her head. "I have sworn to protect him from that."

Green eyes narrowed and flashed. "Nothing is so tedious as maudlin self-sacrifice. Do you love my son?"

"Yes," she whispered.

"Then marry the boy and, for pity's sake, stop looking so tragic. I cannot abide a lovesick fool."

Marry the boy.

"I do love him," Julia said, feeling that love bloom from her center outward, a bittersweet wine that warmed and stung. "Too much to cause him pain."

The bedraggled dragon charged forward, closing the distance between them, halting mere inches away. The old woman's small, slender frame shook with a fine tremor. "What pain do you seek to spare him? You have already broken his heart."

Her words were flat and plain, unadorned by her usual hauteur. This was the dragon stripped of her fire and majesty. This was a mother speaking the truth.

"Where is he?" Julia mouthed the question, unsure if any sound emerged.

"Take the road to Steadwick. If you go now, you may find him."

Her heart was pounding. She glanced back at her dearest friend, who smiled tearfully and nodded. "Go," Helen urged. "Don't forget your cloak."

Apparently, Peggy had been alerted that Julia might be venturing outside. She was standing in the entrance hall with Julia's brown wool cloak draped over her arm. Which was odd, because Julia had made no mention of it.

She had, in fact, raced with unseemly haste.

Peggy promptly draped her cloak around her shoulders and gave her a suspiciously sentimental grin. "Good luck, my lady."

Wasting no time unraveling the mystery, Julia flew through the door into swirls of fluffy white. She could scarcely see three feet in front of her face, so thick was the swarm of tufted flakes.

She could not see far, but she could hear. Amidst the sigh of wind and the cool hush of winter, she heard the snuffle of a horse. Slowly, she took the steps down to the drive, her slippers sinking deep while snow kissed and melted on her ankles and calves.

She didn't feel it.

He was there. A dark figure holding a white horse. Standing in a blizzard. Waiting.

For her.

"Charlie," she breathed.

"She wasn't terribly dramatic, I hope. Mother does love a good show."

He was covered in snow. It clung to his lashes, layered his shoulders, turned his hair white. She wanted to brush her fingers all over him, lay beside him while the fire warmed their naked bodies and melted them into each other.

Above all, she wanted to marry him. "Charlie. I want to marry you."

Silence. Harsh breathing. Then, "Bloody hell, woman."

"I may never give you children." At some point, the melting snow ceased being the only wetness upon her face. "But I will give you my life. Everything I have. If you will make me your wife."

There was a snick as he tossed the reins over his horse's neck. Then he was striding toward her. Purposefully. Swiftly.

And he was kissing her madly, lips and tongue and heat. And she was spinning wildly, lifted and cradled and cherished.

"You are rhyming again, love." He grinned against her mouth.

She laughed. The joy of it spilling out to dance among the snowflakes. She clung to his neck and let it take her.

He cupped her face in his hands. Wiped away the snow and tears. Whispered with heartbreaking tenderness, "Oh, God, Julia. I love you so damn much."

"That is what changed my mind, my darling. I thought I was

protecting you. Instead, I was depriving you of the one thing you deserve most of all—to marry the woman you love and be loved by her so thoroughly that you never feel a moment's regret."

"I am glad you came to your bloody senses."

"Mmm. You will love me, and I will love you. Forever." She smiled. Kissed his substantial chin. "In my estimation, one could not ask for more perfect symmetry."

Chapter Twelve

"Glad tidings, indeed. Perhaps now you may ponder the merits of repetition and happy abundance. And writing your mother with greater frequency. I do like to stay informed."

—The Dowager Marchioness of Wallingham to her son, Charles, upon receiving the most astonishing news.

∞

Twelve days later – December 24, 1818
St. Mary's Church, Steadwick Park, Suffolk

They were married by a man with a lisp. Charlie had tried mightily to obtain red roses, but the only ones he could find were a rather uninspired yellow. The pine boughs that had been joyfully cut that morning to decorate the pews were already shedding their needles, littering the church's stone floors. One week earlier, Helen had come down with a stomach ailment that left her pale and unsteady while acting as Julia's attendant. Lord Dunston's waistcoat was a red so bright, it made Julia's crimson wool gown appear lackluster. Halfway through the ceremony, one of Dunston's dogs—a spaniel, if she did not miss her guess—raced up the aisle to sit panting and whining at Dunston's side.

It was perfect. Every part.

Because all Julia saw was her beloved Charlie, tall and impeccable and shining his love for her from glittering green eyes. All she heard was the music of his words promising to be hers forever. All she knew was that nothing else mattered.

Afterward, as they made their way past the pews to the entrance, her eyes found those of Charlie's mother, now her mother-in-law. The dowager gave her an imperious nod before wrinkling her nose at the spaniel's antics.

Julia tugged Charlie to a stop and held up a finger to ask for a moment. Then, she went to Dorothea Bainbridge, bent close, and kissed her soft, wrinkled cheek.

"Good heavens, girl."

"Thank you," Julia whispered, her eyes welling with everything that was inside her. "Thank you for my Charlie."

A sniff. "Sentimental nonsense." The tone was dismissive, but the hand that squeezed hers said it meant a great deal more than nonsense. "Go on with you, then." The dowager waved them away. "Cake awaits. Let us not dally."

Later, after the ceremony and the cake and several waltzes with her new husband, Julia rocked upon the back of her mare as she and Charlie wound through still, hushed woods. The snow had melted, leaving the cottage surrounded by glistening evergreens.

"Even in the daylight, it still seems magical, does it not?"

Charlie glanced back at her from where he prepared to dismount. One dark brow arched. "If it appears so to you, love."

She grinned. "Come now. Don't be cynical. This place is ours. Therein lies the magic."

He moved to lift her from her horse, his hands fastening around her waist. As he slid her down his front, the friction of her breasts and his chest served as kindling for the coming fire. "Every moment with you is magic, Julia."

She sighed. Melted.

"Especially the naked ones."

Her swat landed on his shoulder. He merely laughed and bent to scoop her into his arms.

She yelped as her feet left the ground. Gripped his neck with flailing arms when he started for the cottage's entrance at a rather determined pace. As he shoved the door open with a grunt, one of her feet snagged on the doorframe, causing Charlie to stumble.

Which caused her to panic for fear that he might drop her.

Which resulted in the dislodging of his hat.

Which he promptly flattened with his boot.

"Bloody hell. That was my best hat."

"Charlie," she breathed, eyes wide, heart pounding. "What did you do?"

"I crushed my favorite hat."

"No, you silly man. The roses. Oh, they're magnificent, Charlie." The room was filled with them. Red roses, lush and dark, in vases on every solid surface and lying strewn upon the bed. They perfumed the air and made her want to cry.

He moved to the chair and sat with her in his lap. "Do they make you happy?"

She buried her face in his neck and nodded, unable to speak.

He kissed her temple. Then her cheek. Then her lips. "Good."

"No, my love," she said, stroking his brow and savoring the warmth of the fire. "Perfect."

Two months later – February 18, 1819
Steadwick Park, Suffolk

HE MUST GET TO HER. THE AIR ITSELF WAS WHITE, THE BLIZZARD harsher, colder, and angrier than anything December had inflicted. But he would push on. Push Ceres faster beneath him. Push Dr. Sutton from his breakfast and his wife and his comfortable house.

Because she needed him. She was ill. And she was not getting better.

A bitter gust clawed its way down his neck. He dug his heels deeper into Ceres's sides. The stallion was his fastest horse, still fractious and a bit unpredictable after fourteen years of breeding champions, but bloody fast.

The physician rode his second fastest horse.

"Keep up!" Charles shouted.

The plump, middle-aged doctor nodded, but appeared to be having trouble maintaining his seat. Reluctantly, Charles slowed their pace. He couldn't have the bloody physician falling and cracking his head. There wasn't another around for miles.

He noted the curve in the drive, the leafless oak tree. They were almost there.

Almost there. Almost there. Almost there.

Julia had tried to calm him before he left. She had tried to tell him to wait until the storm passed to fetch the physician. But this was the eighteenth day she had been ill. Eighteen. Days. And she was worse, not better. Pale. Exhausted by routine tasks. Sleeping more than she was awake. And wretchedly, violently ill several times each day. She hadn't reorganized anything in days. He could not bear it a moment longer.

At last, they arrived in front of Steadwick Hall. Ceres was heaving and damp, as was Dr. Sutton's mount. He did not care. He dragged the man stumbling and flailing from the back of the horse, up the steps, and directly to the chamber where Charles's heart lay dozing, a folded cloth on her forehead, a blue coverlet keeping her warm.

Peggy stood by, wringing her hands. She curtsied when he entered, her eyes wide and fearful.

"Fetch tea," Charles growled.

Peggy squeaked and scuttled away.

The physician shook the snow from his coat and straightened to his full, middling height. "My lord, I shall need a bit of—ahem—privacy with my patient, if you don't mind."

Charles shot him a narrow glare. "You are not to look upon her nakedness."

"B-but I—I must have leave to—"

"This is my wife. The Marchioness of Wallingham. If she worsens or ..." He swallowed, unable to finish the unthinkable thought. "If you do not make her better, I shall rip the last vestiges of hair from your—"

"Charlie." The single breathed word stopped him, pulled his entire being toward the bed. She stretched her hand out toward him, her eyes drowsy but not pained.

He stroked and held that precious hand between his, kissing the knuckles she complained were too pointy. "How are you, love?"

"Vexed."

He blinked. "Why?"

"I told you not to go out in the storm, and yet that is precisely what you did."

"You scarcely leave the bed," he snapped. "And when you do, it is to cast up your accounts. This cannot continue much longer, Julia."

She sighed and squeezed his hand. "You've fetched the physician. Let him do his work."

His jaw tightened. "You wish me to leave the room, do you not?"

"I love you. And yes."

He left. Because she'd asked.

The waiting was agony. He spent the first quarter-hour nursing a cognac in his study, the second quarter-hour pacing the length of the gallery, which ran the entire width of the house. The third quarter-hour, he cornered his butler to inform the man the bloody clocks had malfunctioned. Surely it had been at least half a day since the physician had closed Julia's chamber door and begun "examining" Charles's wife.

Finally, Peggy appeared in the library doorway to inform him that the physician was prepared to discuss his findings. Charles took the stairs two at a time. He hadn't sprinted so since he was a boy clambering over Grimsgate's rocky outcroppings. He tore into the bedchamber, noting Julia's tear-streaked face and the physician's wide grin.

He did not think. He simply grasped the man's cheap cravat and twisted until the portly doctor stood on his toes and turned approximately the color of raspberries.

"Charlie! Stop! Release him at once."

He did. Because she asked.

The man coughed for an absurdly long time.

"Come here, my darling." She held both arms out to him. Propped, as she was, with her back against a series of pillows, she appeared to have more color than before. Perhaps it was his imagination.

He sat gingerly on the edge of the mattress and slid his arms around her back, drawing her gently against him. "What did he do, love? I will see him hanged."

She stroked his hair, his face. "Oh, I think you may change your mind on that score."

Turning a glare on the man still struggling with his cravat, he demanded, "Well, Sutton? What did you find? Can her ailment be eased?"

The doctor nodded and cleared his throat before rasping, "Six months or so."

"Six bloody months? What sort of outrageous quackery is this?"

He expected an answer from Sutton. Instead, Julia said, "Not an ailment. Not an ailment, Charlie."

Her face was wet, the tears flowing freely now.

He held his breath. "Then what?"

"A babe, my lord," replied the doctor, apparently having regained his composure. "Six months or so. As I said."

Charles swiveled to Julia. Then back to the doctor. Then back to Julia.

It could not be. "It cannot be. But, we thought it was—"

"Helen's stomach ailment." She grinned through her tears, her eyes shimmering with red-rimmed joy. "I know. She suffered for more than a fortnight. Dreadful. But it is not an ailment, Charlie. It is ..." She covered her lips with her fingers. "A child."

"But, I thought you were ..."

Her eyes squeezed shut, her hands settling over her belly. When she opened them again, she pierced him clean through. "A child, my love. A child."

The physician intruded to explain that, although the marchioness's history of irregular monthly courses had led *other* physicians to conclude that her difficulties in conceiving were of a permanent nature, he had witnessed many such reversals in his day.

"Bedford physicians," the man huffed. "A presumptuous lot. There is still much we do not understand about why such difficulties arise."

Charles tried to listen. Tried to breathe. But his eyes were riveted upon the spot where Julia's hands lay over her womb. Over his child.

Slowly, he moved his hand to hover above hers, not touching, not daring to believe. She took hold of him, flattened his palm against her belly.

"Bloody hell," he whispered before swallowing the sudden

lump in his throat. "Julia." His eyes flew to hers.

She was smiling. Loving him.

He frowned. "Oh, God."

"What is it?"

"I've only just realized. We will have to inform Mother."

She laughed with such joy, he thought he might weep. Which was unacceptable. So, instead, he kissed her until they were both breathless.

"Well, now," said the physician, opening the door. "Time for me to be off. Rest well, my lady. Try to eat when you can. A bit of mint in your tea will help calm your stomach."

Julia thanked him, but Charles wanted answers. He glowered at the man. "Is that all you can offer to ease her discomfort?"

The physician merely smiled and donned his hat. "You mustn't worry, my lord. Even the worst blizzards run their course. That is what makes spring all the sweeter."

Charles continued glowering at the closed door. "Perfect rubbish," he muttered. "What is a physician's useful purpose if he cannot provide any solution more clever than *mint?*"

Julia chuckled and shook her head. "Oh, Charlie," she sighed. "Now, there is the dragon I adore."

What's beneath the dapper Lord Dunston's flashy waistcoats? Much more than anyone suspects. Uncover all his secrets in Book Seven of the Rescued from Ruin series, available now! Here's a sneak peek:

Confessions of a Dangerous Lord

ELISA BRADEN

Confessions of a Dangerous Lord

※

"The purpose of the season is to attract suitors. The purpose of attracting suitors is to acquire a husband. If you wish to be amused, I suggest acquiring a dog."

—THE DOWAGER MARCHIONESS OF WALLINGHAM to Lady Maureen Huxley regarding said lady's recent loss of composure in the face of Lord Dunston's provocations.

※

March 20, 1819
Mayfair

MAUREEN'S DOWNFALL BEGAN DURING AN OTHERWISE SEDATE quadrille. She was spinning to a stop on the fourth figure of *Le Pantalon*. Henry, the dastardly devil, stood across from her, waggling his brows like a madman.

That was what did it.

She bent double, covering helpless, giggling snorts with one gloved hand while the first couple advanced and retreated between them. Although she was part of the second couple, she could not complete *L'été*. Laughter had possessed her with maniacal force. Violins continued their spirited accompaniment as she gasped rudely and held her middle.

Oh, good heavens. She could not stop. How mortifying.

She glanced across the bewildered, spinning couples to the imp who had prodded her with silly faces and pointed stares at Lord Burnley's prominent backside. Henry grinned back, his handsome features wreathed in wicked satisfaction.

He had wanted this, blast him. Yet even knowing it was true, knowing that her partner for the quadrille, Mr. Hastings, must think her positively mad, she could not stifle herself.

A convulsive hum of laughter escaped her fingers. Her eyes watered. Her ribs ached.

Stop. She must stop. But the memory of Burnley's bum waddling like a drunken duck each time he bounced from one foot to the next, flopping the tails of his coat like a pair of black wings was simply too much to bear.

She could not catch her breath. Turning her back to the other dancers to face the wall of Lady Holstoke's drawing room, she squeezed her waist harder and straightened. She held her breath. Perhaps she would suffocate and be spared the indignity of this moment.

"Bit of a cough. Not to worry. Carry on," Henry called to the other dancers before a masculine hand cupped her lower back brazenly—one might even say possessively, if one were fanciful.

"Oh, God, Henry," she chirped through her fingers. "If you dare speak to me right now, I shall ... st-strike you ..."

"Hmm, let me guess," the devil purred in her ear. "With Lord Burnley's chair? I wager it would deliver a thrashing unmatched by seats of, shall we say, lesser proportions."

Oh, no. Here it came again, bursting from her like champagne from a shaken bottle.

Henry's steady hand steered her through the throng of appalled peers and matrons. At least, she assumed they were appalled. Tears streamed down her cheeks now. Perhaps the moisture would cool them, for she felt the prickling heat of the Huxley Flush. She was a Huxley. Therefore, her cheeks stained red at the slightest provocation.

And there was no greater provocation than Henry Thorpe, the Earl of Dunston.

He ushered her out of the crowd into a dark-paneled corridor.

She collapsed against a wall and covered her hot face before releasing a groan. "Henry, what have you done? You left your partner stranded. Poor Miss Andrews. Oh! And poor Mr. Hastings ..."

"There, there, pet." White-gloved fingers dangled a white square in her vision. "I am certain Hastings will understand. Lord Burnley's *Pantalon* was breathtaking."

Another giggle escaped. This time, she bit her lips between her teeth.

She would *not* start laughing again. She would control herself, dash it all.

Dabbing her cheeks with Henry's offering, she rolled against the wall until she could see him again.

The imp. He was her friend, although at one time, she'd been certain he would be more. Presently, his insouciance was vexing.

He grinned down at her, white teeth flashing in the low light of the tapers behind him. Full of distracting wit, Henry's masculine beauty was easily overlooked. But he was heart-meltingly handsome. Brown hair shone with hints of auburn. A high-bridged, refined nose centered proportionate features. Dancing eyes beckoned one closer, if only to see how dark the color blue could be. Full, smiling lips made a woman picture all the wicked things he might do for hours—even days—if one were the object of his desire.

Maureen was not such an object, of course. He'd taken pains to convey the message gently, but convey it he had.

Now, she tore herself from the beauty of his mouth to sigh and narrow her eyes upon his. "I should pummel you," she gritted. "Have you any idea how long I have waited for Mr. Hastings to approach me?"

"Since you discovered his grandfather's proximity to the hereafter?"

"Three weeks. And my interest is not in his title, you devil."

"Of course not. Must be the hair."

"Mr. Hastings is quite handsome; a broad forehead gives a man an academic air. I find him most appealing."

"Hmm. Broad. Yes. I'm having a bit of trouble with the 'academic' part of your description, however."

She stamped her foot. "Stop being such an aggravation. He may not have your wit, but he is not dim. He attended Cambridge."

A snort. "Precisely."

"Besides, many ladies regard a bit of ... thinning as rather distinguished. I happen to be one."

"Thinning? At this rate, he'll be entirely bald by thirty." He arched a brow. "Perhaps wigs will become fashionable again, and he may spare us the full glare of his rapier intellect."

Leaning back against the paneled wall, she briefly closed her eyes, a familiar ache shuddering in her chest. This was not laughter. This was despair. It had become a constant companion over the past two seasons.

She opened her eyes to find Henry staring down at her. "I must marry someone," she whispered. "Mr. Hastings is ..."

A muscle ticked in his lean jaw. "Not right for you."

"I fear some of us must accept our limitations."

Eyes flaring, raking her face and throat in a way that made her swallow, Henry cocked his head and gave her a faint grin. "What limitations would those be, pet?"

"After three seasons, I have no offers."

He said nothing.

"Something is obviously wrong with me, Henry."

"Don't be silly. You are perfect."

"Really."

"Of course."

"Then explain my failure. Men approach me, they appear to find me pleasing—"

"Naturally."

"And then"—she gave a flailing, forlorn shrug—"they disappear. No more dances. No more drives in their phaetons. No more lovely chats or even the mildest flirtation. I have not been kissed in ages."

His smile faded. He retreated a step.

"No," she said, pushing away from the wall. "Answer me, if you please."

He glanced left then right, giving a polite nod to a white-haired gentleman traveling from the billiard room to the drawing room. "What do you wish me to say?" he murmured.

"I have tried everything." She hated the way her voice contorted. Henry was ever the polished wit. She'd rarely seen him overcome by any emotion stronger than exasperation. Heaven forefend he should suffer a wounded heart's despair, as she had.

"Define 'everything.'" His words were hard, his jaw once again flexing, though his eyes remained turned toward the billiard room.

She wadded his handkerchief then smoothed it between her palms. Truthfully, she would prefer not to reveal all she had done to improve herself. The magnitude of her efforts was embarrassing.

"All I have ever desired is to fall in love. To marry a good man and have a home and children." She chuckled. "*Many* children. What else would you expect from a Huxley girl?"

Finally, his gaze returned to her, heated and strange. He did not smile fondly or utter a charming quip. He said nothing at all, staring down at her and gritting his teeth.

Her confidences were obviously causing him discomfort. Although they had been friends for nearly two years, and their families acquainted for longer, Henry avoided conversations of this sort—intimate and plain—in favor of lighter subjects and droll banter.

However, given that he had spoiled her chances with Mr. Hastings, she felt little remorse. Let him be uncomfortable. She needed answers.

"Something about me repels gentlemen's interest." Firmly, she held his gaze. "I have searched for the cause. I asked my sisters. Mama and Papa. I even asked John what it could be." Her brother had turned crimson before stammering that he was not in a position to judge the womanly appeal of his sister.

Henry's brows arched. "His response?"

"He fled the room as though I had threatened to set his waistcoat ablaze."

"Sensible decision." Henry indicated his own waistcoat with a casual stroke of his finger. It was ornate gold silk, the pride of his expansive collection. He tended to wear it on more formal occasions. "We are not heathens, after all."

She snorted.

He grinned.

For a moment, she remembered why she'd once thought they would share far more than friendship. But that was years ago. Two, to be precise.

Drawing a deep breath, she sallied onward. "Cease distracting me. I require your advice if I am to succeed in my aim."

"Landing Hastings?"

"Or another suitable gentleman. I must determine what is

wrong with me and repair it forthwith. Three seasons constitute an acceptable time frame for a lady in my position. Four would invite pity."

He sighed. "Why me, pet?"

She raised her chin. "We are friends, are we not?"

"Certainly." Caution made the word sound like a question.

"And you are a man."

"You noticed. I am honored."

"As a man—one who might have once looked upon me with some ... admiration?" She swallowed as he gave no response. Not even a blink. "I wish to know what caused your interest to wane. Was it my gowns?" She brushed a hand down the layered canary silk of her skirt. "My hair?" She touched the curls at her temple. "My insistence on discussing Capability Brown's use of serpentine lakes in his landscape improvements?"

Finally, a smile. "None of those. You are lovely. Despite your affection for Mr. Brown's work. A glorified gardener, that one. Any fool can dam a stream and plant a bit of grass."

"Henry."

"Beg your pardon, pet. Do go on."

"I have no more guesses. It cannot be my scent. I have visited Floris numerous times, and the perfumer has attested that, while I might change my scent, there is little to improve upon."

"Has he now?"

"Yes. Furthermore, I have purchased outrageous quantities of honey vanilla soap, violet tooth powder, orange flower hair rinse, and rose milk cold cream. It is more than Papa can bear. He recently set a new budget, and he is earnest in its limitations."

"I can imagine."

"Still, I bathe quite frequently. More so than other young ladies. I am most fond of it."

Henry cleared his throat and rubbed at the corner of his mouth. "Bathing?"

She nodded. "Not the sort with a washstand and cloth, mind you. No, no. *Full* immersion. It is a dreadful lot of hauling water, and I must bribe the footmen regularly, but I *adore* the sensations of heat and wetness and steam surrounding me. Could anything be more pleasurable?"

Again, he was silent, his thumb stroking oddly at the edge of his lower lip.

She shook her head. "In any event, I have determined, after much introspection and experimentation, that my odor is not offensive, and therefore not the cause of my problem."

"I should think not." His voice had gone hoarse and, once again, he avoided her eyes. His gaze now hovered between her throat and midsection. If she didn't know better, she would suspect he was admiring her bosom. Men often did. But not Henry. First of all, it was too dark in the corridor for him to see her properly, even if he were so inclined. Second, he was not so inclined. In fact, he did not regard her as a woman worthy of ogling. His affection was more ... brotherly, perhaps. No, that wasn't quite right either. He and John were acres apart in their disposition toward her.

Dash it all, she did not *know* how he regarded her. Affectionately, warmly, humorously, yes. They enjoyed one another to an absurd degree. No one made her laugh like Henry. And, yet, whatever her feelings for him, his were strictly platonic.

"I chatter too much, don't I?" she blurted, ashamed to utter her darkest suspicion, but sensing she must force both herself and Henry to tend the matter at hand—her inability to hold a man's interest. "Gentlemen find me charming enough for an hour or two, but they tire of hearing me go on and on." She squeezed her eyes closed and straightened her spine. "Tell me truly. I can bear it, but you must be honest, Henry. I must know."

A pair of lean, elegant hands gripped the sides of her shoulders with unexpected firmness. Her eyes popped open. His palms heated her skin through his gloves and the beaded yellow cap sleeves of her gown.

"Listen carefully. There. Is. *Nothing*. Wrong with you."

She opened her mouth to protest.

He gave her a little shake before dropping his hands away. "Nothing. You are perfect in every conceivable sense."

"Of course I am not. Otherwise, I would already be wed. No. I am flawed in some critical aspect only a gentleman would discern. You may hesitate to wound my feelings, but my suffering shall be far lengthier if you do not simply tell me—"

"You choose weak men. Weak and inconstant. That is your problem."

She rolled her eyes. "You would blame *them?* I am the common thread, here, Henry. Me. Perhaps in my first season, I would accept such an answer, but not now. *You* are hardly weak. And *you* do not want me."

He fell back a full step, the ripple of his throat jostling an expertly tied cravat. Several breaths drifted by while his eyes remained locked upon her, flared and glittering.

Oh, dear. Perhaps she had gone too far. She hadn't wanted to toss his rejection in his face so bluntly. Come to that, perhaps describing her love for bathing was a bit much, as well. Conviviality was no excuse for a breach of decorum.

After a time, he spoke. "Let us return to your mother. We have been alone here too long." His lips quirked. "Mustn't set the hounds of gossip upon our heads."

As he pivoted away, she reached to grasp his arm. His violent flinch startled her, and she released him instantly. Chest heaving on fast breaths, he held himself rigid, his muscles flexing in time with his fists.

Yes, she had erred badly.

"I—I am sorry, Henry. I did not mean to disconcert you so."

A moment passed before he grinned over his shoulder in a semblance of his usual fashion. Without humor, it was simply white teeth and a hard jaw. "Never fear, pet. It takes a great deal more than your perfect self to set me off balance." He crooked his right arm and nodded toward the drawing room. "Shall we?"

Want more of Henry and Maureen's story?
Confessions of a Dangerous Lord is available now!
Find it at www.elisabraden.com

More from Elisa Braden

Be first to hear about new releases, price specials, and more—sign up for Elisa's free email newsletter at www.elisabraden.com so you don't miss a thing!

Midnight in Scotland Series
In the enchanting new Midnight in Scotland series, the unlikeliest matches generate the greatest heat. All it takes is a spark of Highland magic.

THE MAKING OF A HIGHLANDER (BOOK ONE)
Handsome adventurer John Huxley is locked in a land dispute in the Scottish Highlands with one way out: Win the Highland Games. When the local hoyden Mad Annie Tulloch offers to train him in exchange for "Lady Lessons," he agrees. But teaching the fiery, foul-mouthed, breeches-wearing lass how to land a lord seems impossible—especially when he starts dreaming of winning her for himself.

THE TAMING OF A HIGHLANDER (BOOK TWO)
Wrongfully imprisoned and tortured, Broderick MacPherson lives for one purpose—punishing the man responsible. When a wayward lass witnesses his revenge, he risks returning to the prison that nearly killed him. Kate Huxley has no wish to testify against a man who's already suffered too much. But the only remedy is to become his wife. And she can't possibly marry such a surly, damaged man…can she?

Rescued from Ruin Series
Discover the scandalous predicaments, emotional redemptions, and gripping love stories (with a dash of Lady Wallingham) in the scorching series that started it all!

EVER YOURS, ANNABELLE (PREQUEL)
As a girl, Annabelle Huxley chased Robert Conrad with reckless abandon, and he always rescued her when she pushed too far—until the accident that cost him everything. Seven years later, Robert discovers the girl with the habit of chasing trouble is now a siren he can't resist. But when a scandalous secret threatens her life, how far will he go to rescue her one last time?

THE MADNESS OF VISCOUNT ATHERBOURNE (BOOK ONE)
Victoria Lacey's life is perfect—perfectly boring. Agree to marry a lord who has yet to inspire a single, solitary tingle? It's all in a day's work for the oh-so-proper sister of the Duke of Blackmore. Surely no one suspects her secret longing for head-spinning passion. Except a dark stranger, on a terrace, at a ball where she should not be kissing a man she has just met. Especially one bent on revenge.

THE TRUTH ABOUT CADS AND DUKES (BOOK TWO)
Painfully shy Jane Huxley is in a most precarious position, thanks to dissolute charmer Colin Lacey's deceitful wager. Now, his brother, the icy Duke of Blackmore, must make it right, even if it means marrying her himself. Will their union end in frostbite? Perhaps. But after lingering glances and devastating kisses, Jane begins to suspect the truth: Her duke may not be as cold as he appears.

Desperately Seeking a Scoundrel (Book Three)
Where Lord Colin Lacey goes, trouble follows. Tortured and hunted by a brutal criminal, he is rescued from death's door by the stubborn, fetching Sarah Battersby. In return, she asks one small favor: Pretend to be her fiancé. Temporarily, of course. With danger nipping his heels, he knows it is wrong to want her, wrong to agree to her terms. But when has Colin Lacey ever done the sensible thing?

The Devil Is a Marquess (Book Four)
A walking scandal surviving on wits, whisky, and wicked skills in the bedchamber, Benedict Chatham must marry a fortune or risk ruin. Tall, redheaded disaster Charlotte Lancaster possesses such a fortune. The price? One year of fidelity and sobriety. Forced to end his libertine ways, Chatham proves he is more than the scandalous charmer she married, but will it be enough to keep his unwanted wife?

When a Girl Loves an Earl (Book Five)
Miss Viola Darling always gets what she wants, and what she wants most is to marry Lord Tannenbrook. James knows how determined the tiny beauty can be—she mangled his cravat at a perfectly respectable dinner before he escaped. But he has no desire to marry, less desire to be pursued, and will certainly not kiss her kissable lips until they are both breathless, no matter how tempted he may be.

Twelve Nights as His Mistress (Novella - Book Six)
Charles Bainbridge, Lord Wallingham, spent two years wooing Julia Willoughby, yet she insists they are a dreadful match destined for misery. Now, rather than lose her, he makes a final offer: Spend twelve nights in his bed, and if she can deny they are perfect for each other, he will let her go. But not before tempting tidy, sensible Julia to trade predictability for the sweet chaos of true love.

Confessions of a Dangerous Lord (Book Seven)
Known for flashy waistcoats and rapier wit, Henry Thorpe, the Earl of Dunston, is deadlier than he appears. For years, his sole focus has been hunting a ruthless killer through London's dark underworld. Then Maureen Huxley came along. To keep her safe, he must keep her at arm's length. But as she contemplates marrying another man, Henry's caught in the crossfire between his mission and his heart.

Anything but a Gentleman (Book Eight)
Augusta Widmore must force her sister's ne'er-do-well betrothed to the altar, or her sister will bear the consequences. She needs leverage only one man can provide—Sebastian Reaver. When she invades his office demanding a fortune in markers, he exacts a price a spinster will never pay—become the notorious club owner's mistress. And when she calls his bluff, a fiery battle for surrender begins.

A Marriage Made in Scandal (Book Nine)
As the most feared lord in London, the Earl of Holstoke is having a devil of a time landing a wife. When a series of vicious murders brings suspicion to his door, only one woman is bold enough to defend him—Eugenia Huxley. Her offer to be his alibi risks scandal, and marriage is the remedy. But as a poisonous enemy coils closer, Holstoke finds his love for her might be the greatest danger of all.

A Kiss from a Rogue (Book Ten)
A cruel past left Hannah Gray with one simple longing—a normal life with a safe, normal husband. Finding one would be easy if she weren't distracted by wolf-in-rogue's-clothing Jonas Hawthorn. He's tried to forget the haughty Miss Gray. But once he tastes the heat and longing hidden beneath her icy mask, the only mystery this Bow Street man burns to solve is how a rogue might make Hannah his own.

About the Author

Reading romance novels came easily to Elisa Braden. Writing them? That took a little longer. After graduating with degrees in creative writing and history, Elisa spent entirely too many years in "real" jobs writing T-shirt copy ... and other people's resumes ... and articles about gift-ware displays. But that was before she woke up and started dreaming about the very *unreal* job of being a romance novelist. Better late than never.

Elisa lives in the gorgeous Pacific Northwest, where you're constitutionally required to like the colors green and gray. Good thing she does. Other items on the "like" list include cute dogs, strong coffee, and epic movies. Of course, her favorite thing of all is hearing from readers who love her characters as much as she does. If you're one of those, get in touch on Facebook and Twitter or visit **www.elisabraden.com**.

Printed in Great Britain
by Amazon